A Long Shadow

A LONG SHADOW

A CHIEF INSPECTOR SHADOW MYSTERY

H L Marsay

TULE
PUBLISHING

DEDICATION

To my mum, Rita and my dad, John.
I am so lucky to have such wonderful parents.
Thank you for all your love and support xx.

ACKNOWLEDGEMENTS

Thanks so much to everyone at the incredible Tule Publishing: Jane Porter, Meghan Farrell, Cyndi Parent and Nikki Babri—you all made my dream come true.

I am so grateful to the amazing team of editors for their advice, encouragement and guidance:

Sinclair Sawhney, Helena Newton and Marlene Engel.

Many thanks also to Lee Hyat for coordinating the perfect book cover.

CHAPTER ONE

YORK, THE ANCIENT capital of the north. A city that was once attacked by marauding Scots and pillaging Viking hordes, now found itself besieged most weekends by drunken stag and hen parties. They came armed with inappropriate inflatables and L plates rather than axes and swords, but still caused chaos and sometimes bloodshed. So, early one bright spring morning, as the sun was beginning to rise and while most of the city was still slumbering, York's street-cleaning teams were busy at work. Sweeping and hosing away the mess and debris left behind by the revellers, who had thronged the streets only a few hours earlier.

The team assigned to Goodramgate and Petergate that morning was Brian Elliot and his apprentice Ross Jones. Brian, as the senior of the two, retained control of the power washer whilst directing Ross to collect half-eaten, congealing kebabs and the odd abandoned high heel or discarded joke wig. They were both relieved not to have been sent to Micklegate, the street most popular with the visiting hens and stags from the northeast, who challenged themselves to drink in every pub on the street and therefore complete 'The Micklegate Run.' This morning, Brian and Ross began working in the shadow of the city walls making their way past cafes, shops and hair salons towards the Minster. Their progress was occasionally impeded by finding one of the doorways occupied.

"Wakey, wakey! Rise and shine!" Brian called, cheerfully to a loosely constructed cardboard shelter, under the Tudor gable of the National Trust Shop. The angry head of a black-and-white spaniel emerged, barking furiously. It was followed by a nicotine-stained hand, the middle finger raised in greeting.

"Morning, Jake; morning, Missy!" replied Brian. He headed across the street to Catania's restaurant, where in the covered entrance of Bedern, lay a bundle of sleeping bags. The only visible sign of the bundle's occupant was the long, blonde hair spilling out of the top.

"Come on, love, time to make a move," Brian called out. There was no response. He tried again, a little more loudly. Still nothing. Gently, he nudged the sleeping bags with his foot, then jumped back in horror. A lifeless hand flopped out of the bundle, releasing a half-empty bottle of vodka that fell and smashed on to the pavement.

A LITTLE LATER over in St Helen's Square, Bettys—York's oldest and most famous tearooms—was beginning to serve breakfast. Detective Chief Inspector John Shadow was enjoying a full English, as he did every morning, whilst silently studying the *Yorkshire Post* crossword.

Across 1 (8 letters)
Wishing they had Sarah's luck, initially makes Jane, Emily and Anne feel lousy

A middle-aged man in a dark suit with black, slightly greying hair and bright blue eyes, he went largely unnoticed by the other diners. He sat at his usual corner table. With his back to the room, he was still able to glance up occasionally and observe the chattering customers and bustling waitresses, reflected in the mirror running along the wall in front of him. It was in this mirror that he now spotted a familiar tall, thin figure in a black leather jacket hurrying across St Helen's Square towards the tearooms. Shadow sighed. Sergeant Jimmy Chang may only have been working for him for a few weeks, but surely he knew enough not to interrupt him when he was eating. Barnfather, his previous assistant, would have known to wait outside until he'd finished. Unfortunately, Barnfather had emigrated to New Zealand and was now an inspector in Invercargill. The joke back at the station was that as Antarctica didn't have a police force, it was the furthest he could go to get away from Shadow.

It wasn't so much that Shadow was a difficult man, more a man of contradictions. He loved food but hated to cook. He shunned the company of others, including his colleagues, but often noticed the smallest detail regarding those around him. For example, he did not know the name of the petite, dark-haired waitress, who served him every morning, but he did know that a month ago she stopped wearing her wedding ring. Also, since then, her eyes had acquired permanent dark shadows beneath them.

As he predicted, in less than a minute, his new sergeant was swiftly weaving through tables and chairs towards him. With his ready smile, he cheerfully apologised to waitresses along the way, before sliding into the seat opposite the inspector.

"Morning, Chief!" he said brightly, seemingly unaware his arrival was less than welcome.

"Sit down, why don't you?" muttered Shadow, biting into a slice of toast.

"Unexplained death, sir. Body found first thing this morning," announced the sergeant, in a loud, clear voice.

The elderly couple at the next table halted their conversation abruptly and turned to stare. Shadow raised his hand to silence his deputy and nodded an apology to his neighbours. He looked at the young man opposite him, so eager and full of enthusiasm. He reminded him of a Labrador puppy he had once owned, when he was a boy. As he recalled, the puppy had been impossible to house-train and he'd spent most of his summer holidays cleaning up his mess.

"Sergeant, where are we?" he asked, lowering his voice so it was almost a whisper. The young man frowned slightly as he glanced around.

"Bettys, sir."

"That's right, one of our city's more refined establishments. Where tourists and locals alike come to enjoy the excellent food and superb service. Perhaps they are even here to celebrate a special occasion. What they are not here to do, is listen to whatever grisly news you are about to impart. Whoever has been found is already dead; you can wait to tell me about them when we get outside."

"Yes, sir," replied Jimmy. Looking a little crestfallen, he leaned forward, his keen dark eyes trying to peer at the crossword. The chief inspector promptly folded the newspaper with a glare. It was bad enough Jimmy spoiling his breakfast, without interfering with ten across too. Shadow raised his hand and called for the bill, before forking the last of the bacon and sausage into his mouth.

When the two men stepped outside, Shadow pulled on his battered, green wax jacket and tucked his newspaper into one of the deep pockets. He could sense his deputy almost straining on the lead.

"Off you go then," he said, with a sigh. Jimmy immediately clicked open his ever-present electronic notebook. Shadow groaned inwardly. He couldn't understand the need for these new-fangled devices. What was wrong with using the old paper notebooks? They cost next to nothing and they never needed to be recharged. Jimmy cleared his throat and began to read.

"Fay Lawton, nineteen years old, female, Caucasian."

Shadow rolled his eyes. "Just say white—we're not American and I can tell she's female if she's called Fay."

"Yes, sir." Jimmy continued, unperturbed, "No fixed abode, no previous convictions, but known to social services. She had a history of drug and alcohol abuse and was found at the entrance to Bedern by two of the council's street cleaners, at approximately 6.10am. Actually, I was the first officer on the scene, sir," he added with a hint of pride. "I heard the ambulance arrive, just as I was about to go out for a run."

Jimmy lived on Goodramgate, above the restaurant his family owned. The Golden Dragon was the city's best Chinese and to Shadow's mind, his new sergeant's only saving grace.

"Good for you, Sergeant," he replied sarcastically, as they set off towards the murder scene. "Cause of death?"

"No obvious injuries, but she still had a bottle of vodka in her hand when she died."

The two men made their way down Stonegate, trying to avoid delivery vans rushing to unload their goods before ten thirty, when the city became a traffic-free zone. They then turned into Deangate. The day's first camera-toting tourists were already swarming towards the Minster. Jimmy swerved and dodged as he attempted not to bomb their photos, but at six foot two and with his long arms and legs, he just seemed to get in the way even more. Shadow kept his head down and stuck to his path regardless. If he stopped every time a tourist wanted to take a picture in York, he'd never get anywhere.

A few moments later, they arrived at the crime scene, cordoned off by uniformed officers as the forensic team carried out their work. Shadow and Jimmy ducked under the police tape and one of the officers lifted the blue cover so Shadow could see the body. He studied her face. She was a pretty girl and looked younger than nineteen. Faint traces of make-up were streaked around her eyes, but her face was also unusually pink and blotchy. She was dressed in jeans, a white vest and a checked shirt that looked several sizes too big. Each ear had been pierced several times, there were two small stars tattooed on her wrist and all her fingernails were bitten down to the skin. Shadow had seen enough. He waved to the officer to cover her again and turned to Jimmy.

"What happened to the bottle of vodka?"

"It got smashed, fell out of her hand when she was found apparently. Forensics are going to do their best, they've already taken the remains away," Jimmy explained as he consulted his electronic notebook.

Shadow nodded. "And who did you say found the body?"

Jimmy scrolled back through the pages before replying. "Brian Elliot, age fifty-eight. He's lived in York all his life and has worked for the council as a street cleaner for the last fifteen years. He's waiting to speak to you, Chief." Jimmy pointed to where a grey-haired man in overalls was sitting on a bench opposite the Minster, puffing on a cigarette. "There was another younger guy with him, Ross Jones, but I'm not sure where he is now, sir. Oh, and a homeless guy, who didn't give his name, but he did identify the deceased. He disappeared before I could get any details."

Shadow groaned in exasperation. "For crying out loud, Jimmy! Evidence smashed, witnesses going missing! You need to get a grip on things, especially seeing as you were the first officer on the scene. Now, go and tell uniform to get the body moved as soon as forensics are done, or we'll have tour parties coming by taking photos—it's a miracle the press isn't here already. Then try to trace her next of kin, if she has any."

Leaving a dejected-looking Jimmy, Shadow stalked over to Brian and introduced himself.

"I understand you and your colleague found the body, Mr Elliot." Brian nodded and Shadow noticed the hand holding his cigarette was trembling.

"Ross? Yes, I told the lad to go home. He was a bit shaken up. He's only been on the job two weeks and it turns out he knew the girl."

Shadow sat down next to him. "Really?"

"They were at primary school together. He didn't recognise her. To tell the truth, I think he tried not to look, you know." Brian paused and rubbed the back of his hand across his eyes. "Then Jake told that Chinese lad her name and Ross said he remembered her."

"Jake?"

"Homeless bloke, you must have seen him around. He's usually hanging about in Museum Gardens. Always has a spaniel with him that looks like she wants to rip your arm off."

Shadow did know him. He thanked Mr Elliot and stood up to leave, but Brian still seemed to want to talk.

"Was it drugs?" he asked.

"We won't know until after the post-mortem, Mr Elliot."

Brian took a last long drag from his cigarette. "I've got a granddaughter about the same age. What a waste. It makes you sick doesn't it?"

As Shadow walked away, he found it difficult not to agree. He'd been in the police for over thirty-five years, but he never got used to seeing a dead body. Now, less than fifteen minutes in, this case was already making him feel ill. He wasn't sure if he should put his indigestion down to rushing his breakfast, having to walk at Jimmy's pace all the way down here, or the sight of yet another wasted young life. He headed down Goodramgate towards Church Street and on the way, called in at the mini supermarket. He picked up a packet of antacid tablets and went through the palaver of buying a packet of cigarettes and matches from behind the newly installed curtain. Then he took a short detour down

Shambles to buy three still-warm pork pies. The mobile phone in his pocket buzzed. He fished it out and squinted at the screen. It was a text from Jimmy to say the body had now been moved. He flicked the phone off. The last thing he needed was minute-by-minute updates interrupting his thoughts.

He eventually found Jake and Missy by the war memorial on Duncombe Place. Jake, an ex-soldier, was dressed as always, in combat trousers and a camouflage T-shirt. He was smoking a rolled-up cigarette, as he sat cross-legged on his folded sleeping bag, reading a tattered Dan Brown paperback. Missy was curled up next to him. Shadow reckoned Jake must have been sleeping on the streets for at least five years.

They had first crossed paths when Jake had rescued Missy from her previous owner, who thought it amusing to stub cigarettes out on the puppy. Jake had taken exception to this and punched the owner unconscious, in the middle of a packed betting shop on Ebor Day. Shadow had been the first officer to attend, as most of uniform were on duty at the racecourse. He had persuaded the furious and bloodied owner to allow Jake to keep the dog and not press charges, on the understanding they would not be charging him with animal cruelty.

Jake had never caused the police any real trouble since, except for receiving the occasional complaint about his companion's aggressive behaviour. Missy may have looked like she was asleep, but as Shadow approached, she suddenly leapt up and began barking furiously.

"Oh, calm down, you," he said, tossing one of the pork pies to the spaniel, who leapt up and caught it expertly, before quickly devouring it. Shadow placed the other pies, cigarettes and matches on the sleeping bag next to Jake. He slowly lowered himself on to the plinth surrounding the memorial to "the glorious dead" of the Boer War. Jake glanced down at the offerings by his side.

"I roll my own," he said stubbornly, taking a drag on the thin cigarette he had balanced between his thumb and finger.

Shadow grinned. "Think of all the time having those will save you, in your busy schedule," he replied.

Jake snorted and came as close as he ever did to smiling. "Yeh, right."

"Well, you certainly left Goodramgate in a hurry earlier. Were you late for an important appointment?" the chief inspector continued.

"I wasn't going to hang about and give you lot the chance to frame me."

Now it was Shadow's turn to give a snort of derision. "What are we going to frame you for? It's got all the signs of a classic overdose hasn't it?"

"Who ODs on half a bottle of voddy?" countered Jake, scornfully raising an eyebrow.

Shadow silently noted his reaction, then changed tack. "Did you know her well?"

Jake took another long drag on his cigarette and shook his head. "No, she was just a kid. She hung around with Ryan and his lot. Most nights she stayed at The Haven."

"So, did she say why she was out on the street last night?"

"Yes, I popped over to borrow a cup of sugar and she told me all about it," he said sarcastically.

Shadow frowned.

"Look," Jake continued, "we turned up at about two in the morning, when the clubs had closed, and all the drunks had buggered off home. I think, only think mind, Fay was across the way, but I didn't speak to her, or see anyone else before you ask. All right?"

"All right," agreed Shadow. He pulled himself up— relieved to leave the cold, hard plinth—and turned to go, when something occurred to him.

"Why were you on Goodramgate anyway? Don't you usually stay in Museum Gardens?" he asked. Jake flicked the stub of his cigarette away and turned his attention to the bag containing the pies.

"They're doing up the Hospitium and the builders have put up barricades. You can't get along the path to the bridge now."

Shadow nodded at the explanation and left the two of them. When he looked back a few seconds later and saw Jake sharing the remaining pies with Missy, he gave a sigh of regret. He should have held on to one. When his stomach calmed down it would have been a welcome mid-morning snack. He made his way along St Leonard's Place, deciding he may as well head towards The Haven and see if the people there could shed any light on what had happened to the dead girl.

THE HAVEN WAS a shelter for the homeless, situated just off Bootham between the city walls and St John's, the city's oldest independent school. The shelter had been opened by Susie Slater, a local girl, who had briefly found fame as a pop star, via a TV talent show nearly thirty years ago. Shadow could quite clearly recall her being on the television and in the newspapers, when he was a young constable down in London. When she retired and returned permanently to her home city, she remained a minor celebrity, called upon whenever a supermarket or nightclub needed opening.

A couple of decades later, when the hit singles were only a distant memory to most people, she and her partner, Luke Carrington, decided to announce in the local press that they wanted to give something back to the city where they had both grown up. They turned Luke's family home, a large four-storey house with a long garden running down towards the river, into The Haven. By all accounts, The Haven was a success. The police were rarely called out there, and Susie and Luke worked with the residents to get them help for their problems and had even managed to get some of them into work.

As Shadow walked down Bootham, dodging a wave of tourists disembarking from their coach, he heard the now-familiar sound of soft feet running up behind him. Although he made a point of not answering his mobile and rarely responded to texts or voicemail, his new sergeant seemed to have an uncanny ability to track him down.

"Yes, Jimmy, what is it?" he asked, without turning around.

"I've got an update, sir," replied the younger man, easily falling into step alongside his boss. "Fay Lawton has no next of kin. Her father is unknown; her mother was in and out of prison for most of her life but died of a drug overdose five years ago. Fay was raised mainly by her maternal grandmother, but she died of a stroke three years ago. That's when Fay became homeless and she's been fending for herself ever since."

Shadow nodded at the sad, but predictable information. It was a familiar story for many of those living on the streets.

"I've spoken to Jake. According to him, Fay spent most nights at The Haven. Let's see if anyone there can tell us why she didn't stay there last night. Any news on the post-mortem? Who's on duty?"

"Donaldson, sir," Jimmy replied with a grimace.

Shadow rolled his eyes. Two pathologists worked for North Yorkshire Police and they could not have been more different. Sophie Newton was in her thirties and from

Newcastle. She was diligent, helpful and in possession of a decent sense of humour. Donaldson, however, was arrogant, pompous and treated each unexplained death he was presented with as a personal inconvenience. He had been threatening to retire for years and as far as Shadow was concerned, that day couldn't come soon enough.

"His secretary told me he would only speak to the chief investigating officer," Jimmy continued. Shadow laughed ruefully.

"Well aren't I the lucky one?" As they turned the corner away from the traffic and on to Marygate, he glanced down and scrutinised what his deputy was wearing. Jimmy, as ever, was dressed in jeans, trainers and a leather jacket.

"Have you ever thought of dressing a little more formally, Sergeant?" he enquired. Jimmy, who was gradually becoming used to his boss's almost constant flow of criticism, lowered the zip of his jacket a couple of inches.

"I'm wearing a shirt and tie underneath, sir, but trainers are good, you know, in case I need to chase after someone."

Shadow shook his head. He couldn't recall the last time he'd needed to chase a suspect.

THE HAVEN WAS in the middle of a row of tall Georgian terrace houses and from the outside, looked no different to its neighbours. Black iron railings ran along the front and several stone steps led up from the street to the imposing dark blue front door. Shadow was surprised to find it swung open automatically when they approached. They stepped into the narrow hallway and walked through a short corridor that led to the reception area. The modern way it had been furnished jarred with the original tiled floor and the elegant staircase leading upstairs. With its pale wooden desk and brightly coloured sofas, it looked like it could belong to any hostel or budget hotel. Only the noticeboard covered in posters for the Samaritans and leaflets for various drug and alcohol rehabilitation agencies gave a clue as to what the place really was.

Behind the desk, a young receptionist with bright pink hair and a nose piercing looked like she had recently been crying. She managed a small smile when she saw Shadow and Jimmy approach, but her eyes filled with tears again, when they explained they were there to ask about Fay. Between loud sniffs, she managed to direct them to the garden at the back of the property, where she told them they would find Susie Slater, who had been on duty the previous night.

They walked down another short corridor and through the back door that was propped open with a small stone Buddha. The garden was surprisingly large for a house so close to the city centre and was surrounded by a high brick wall on the remaining three sides.

Susie was sitting alone on a swing seat in the shade of a blossoming cherry tree, with a pair of gardening gloves and secateurs laying by her side. Shadow recognised her immediately. She hardly seemed to have changed since her days as a pop star. Her long blonde hair was still piled messily on top of her head and her pale blue eyes, with perhaps a few extra creases at the corners, were still heavily lined with kohl. She was wearing slim-fitting jeans, a long white embroidered shirt, and on her arms were many thin silver bangles that jangled when she rose to greet the two policemen.

Shadow made the introductions and followed her as she led them through the flower beds and past the vegetable patch to a small wooden table with four chairs.

"Do sit down, gentlemen, please. May I offer you a glass of lemonade?"

She gave a discreet wave and Shadow turned to see the pink-haired girl slowly carrying a tray with three glasses and a jug of lemonade across the lawn. She placed the tray on the table without a word and then turned and walked back to the house, wiping her eyes with the sleeve of her hoodie as she went.

"Thank you, Jess," Susie called after her, before turning her attention back to Jimmy and Shadow.

"I expect you are here to ask about poor Fay." Her voice was soft and sad as she poured out three drinks.

"You know about Fay already?" asked Shadow, as he accepted the glass with a smile.

"It's a small city, Chief Inspector, and unfortunately bad news travels quickly. Do you know yet what happened?"

"We won't know exactly until after the post-mortem. I understand she usually stayed here."

"Yes, most nights since her grandmother died."

"She had no other family?"

"I'm afraid not, Chief Inspector. The people here were probably the closest thing she had to family. I like to think that she thought of this place as a sort of home from home."

"So why wasn't she here last night?"

"There was a row." Susie paused and took a sip of lemonade, as if trying to carefully choose her words. "Fay was involved with Ryan, one of our other part-time residents. Yesterday, Ryan's ex-girlfriend, Kayleigh was released from prison. At first, all was fine. The three of them met up and went out to celebrate at Ted's Bar, but then things got a little messy. There was an argument. Apparently, Ryan took Kayleigh's side, so Fay was upset. She came here, but she couldn't possibly stay. She was obviously quite drunk, and we have a very strict no drugs or alcohol policy."

"Did Fay have a problem with drugs or alcohol? Was she receiving treatment?" asked Shadow.

Susie shook her head and her long silver earrings sparkled in the sun.

"Not as far as I know. I suppose you could say she had dabbled in the past. However, Fay was easily led. You see she was quite young for her age, trusting and impressionable."

"This lemonade is really good," interrupted Jimmy, as he drained his glass. Shadow scowled at him, but Susie beamed.

"Thank you, Sergeant, I'm pleased you enjoyed it. We grow the lemons here in the greenhouse. We're trying to be as self-sufficient as possible. Almost all the fruit and vegetables we eat here are grown in this garden—apples, pears, carrots, tomatoes, all sorts of things. The residents sometimes help out. I think they find it therapeutic. We even have our own chickens, Bianca, Marianne and Jerry with Mick the cockerel of course." She laughed, and Shadow smiled politely at the joke. Jimmy looked blank and Shadow sensed he was about to ask for an explanation, until he caught his eye and gave a slight, but firm shake of his head.

"Can you tell me what time Fay left here, Miss Slater?" he asked. Susie frowned and thought for a moment.

"We always lock the front door at eleven and she arrived just before then. As I said, she was upset. I tried to calm her down, but when I said she couldn't stay, she took off. I'm not sure, but it was probably about ten past eleven."

"Would it be possible to speak with Mr Carrington too?"

"I'm sorry, he's not here right now. He's out collecting supplies for our soup kitchen."

"You do that as well as running this place? That's very admirable, Miss Slater."

Susie shrugged and gave a sad smile. "Oh do please call me Susie—everybody does." She paused to refill Jimmy's glass. "And the soup kitchen really isn't much bother, but there are so many out on the streets who can't come here because of their addictions; the least we can do is make sure they have a decent meal a couple of times a week. We hold it every Tuesday and Saturday at 6pm in Kings Square."

"How many inmates do you usually have staying here?" Shadow asked.

Susie raised an eyebrow in mock horror and wagged her finger at the policemen.

"Now, now, Chief Inspector, they are our residents, not inmates, and we can take a maximum of eight." Her tone was light-hearted and teasing, but Shadow still inclined his head apologetically.

"Do you and Mr Carrington stay on site too?"

"No, when Luke inherited the property, he was adamant he didn't want to live here."

Shadow glanced back towards the house and wondered why someone wouldn't want to live in such a lovely house with its graceful interiors and beautiful garden.

"You don't have any issues with security?" he asked.

"Not so far, Chief Inspector. We ask our residents to sign in and then out in the morning—that's it. After all, there has to be an element of trust, don't you think?"

Shadow was not trusting by nature, but he decided it was probably not the time to mention this. The two policemen stood to leave, and Susie escorted them back through the house to the front door. There was now no sign of Jess at the reception desk.

"Thank you for your time and for the lemonade, Miss Slater." Shadow and Jimmy both shook her hand.

"Not at all, Chief Inspector, do let me know if there is any more news about poor Fay."

"Of course." Shadow agreed as he walked through the automatic door.

THE TWO POLICEMEN left behind the peace and tranquillity of Marygate and stepped back out into the traffic and noise of Bootham. Shadow thought what an appropriate name The Haven had. In fact, to Fay and to the others who stayed there, it must seem like heaven. He would have liked to have discovered more about Fay and to have spoken to the girl with the pink hair, but perhaps it was better to wait for the results of the post-mortem.

"Right, time for lunch, I think," he announced, as they strode back towards the city walls. Jimmy glanced at his watch. It was barely noon.

"It's a bit early for me, Chief."

Shadow shook his head. He was deeply suspicious of how little his sergeant seemed to eat. As far as he could tell he spent the day fuelled by nothing but chewing gum and takeaway coffees.

"Well I'm eating now. I certainly won't feel like it after I've seen Donaldson."

Shadow was notoriously squeamish. "Why don't you track down the missing street cleaner from this morning?"

"Do you think we're looking at more than an overdose, sir?"

"Probably not, but something Jake said this morning is bothering me," Shadow replied without further elaboration. "I'll be in here if you need me."

With that he stopped abruptly and stepped into the entrance of The Lamb and Lion, leaving his sergeant alone on the pavement.

CHAPTER TWO

Across 7 (5 letters)
Vote often despite Kremlin's authority—that's the spirit!

I**T WAS LATER** in the afternoon when Shadow and Jimmy met again on the other side of the city, at the mortuary. Shadow arrived first, closely followed by his deputy, to receive the results of the post-mortem from Donaldson. Miss Habbershaw, his fearsome secretary had informed them the doctor would be available from two o'clock, so Shadow had automatically added on an hour; however, it was now quarter past three and there was still no sign of Donaldson.

"Did you find our errant young street sweeper?" he asked irritably, as they waited together in the corridor.

"Yes, sir," replied Jimmy, promptly scrolling through the screen of his electronic notebook. "Ross Jones lives in Holgate with his mother and grandfather, who suffers from multiple sclerosis. He's been employed by the council as a street cleaner for exactly twelve days. Prior to that he worked at Speedy Peppers a takeaway pizza place, just off Nunnery Lane. He was at primary school with Fay, then secondary, not that she was there very much. He hadn't seen her since he left school three years ago. This morning, he didn't really get a good look at her or notice anything unusual around where she was found. In fact, he didn't realise it was Fay, until he heard Jake tell me her name. He left as soon as Brian, his boss, said he could."

Jimmy flicked his notebook off and closed it. Before Shadow could ask any further questions, a door opened at the end of the corridor. Donaldson appeared and waved them through to where the body was. Shadow shivered as he stepped inside. Everything about the room was cold, from the artificially low temperature, to the clinical white tiles and the stark fluorescent lights.

"Good afternoon, Chief Inspector," said Donaldson. He looked Jimmy up and down, but didn't bother to acknowledge him, although Shadow had introduced them several times before.

"Didn't you chaps always used to wear a suit and tie? Are standards slipping in CID?" he asked in his slightly sneering tone.

"Times are changing," replied Shadow, smoothly. "The new generation of officers need to be able to respond to the modern challenges of policing, not look like old duffers like you and me."

Jimmy looked surprised to hear Shadow defending him, but Donaldson scowled. He prided himself on his appearance. When not in scrubs, he always wore a three-piece suit with a handkerchief folded neatly in his top pocket.

"Well for once, Shadow, it seems you haven't been completely wasting my time."

Shadow didn't bother to respond. He had always suspected Donaldson was a frustrated thespian and it was much easier to wait and allow him to deliver his well-prepared lines uninterrupted.

"Your vagrant didn't overdose, she was poisoned."

"Really?" asked Jimmy. Donaldson ignored him.

"Specifically, a cyanogenic compound, or in layman's terms, cyanide. It was almost certainly in the vodka she drank. The time of death was approximately one o'clock in the morning." Donaldson then pulled back the blue sheet covering the body with a flourish. "You can quite clearly see the red mottled marks on her face, a classic sign that cyanide was involved."

Shadow hung back considering the pathologist's information, while Jimmy leaned in for a closer look. Shadow did not need to look at the body again. He could clearly remember the unusual blotches from this morning and had no desire to see what was on the slab, after Donaldson had done his work.

"How quickly would the cyanide have killed her?" he asked.

"A mere matter of minutes."

"Had she taken any drugs?"

"No. The blood alcohol count was high, but not fatally so. She had probably been drinking earlier in the day, but she hadn't eaten, her stomach was empty."

"Any sign of assault?"

"If by that you mean, did someone force her to drink the poison? I would say no, she drank of her own volition."

"So, it could be suicide?" asked Jimmy. Shadow was about to reply, when Donaldson scoffed at the idea and gave Jimmy a patronising smile.

"Rather an elaborate way for someone like her to go about taking her own life, Sergeant. Lacing her vodka with cyanide? I'm sure there are more readily available toxins she could have got her hands on. Or why not throw herself into the river or under a train for that matter?"

"But it's still a possibility we can't rule out yet," interjected Shadow, despairing at the pathologist's callousness.

THE TWO POLICE officers left Donaldson as soon as they could, eager to get away from both the person and the place.

"You'd better get on to forensics and find out everything you can about that vodka. We need to find out where it came from and who might have bought it. In the meantime, tell uniform to get in touch with the publicans and bar managers. They need to be warned that there could be a batch of dodgy vodka in the city. Find out if any of them have been approached."

"I'm on it, sir," replied Jimmy, as he almost bounded

away. Shadow watched him go and smiled to himself.

"If he had a tail, he'd be wagging it," he murmured. He couldn't fault his new sergeant's enthusiasm, and professional pride meant he certainly wasn't going to let Donaldson's rudeness towards Jimmy go unchecked. How he'd managed to put up working with that obnoxious doctor for so long was a miracle.

SHADOW DECIDED TO take the long route home. He wandered down Blossom Street, past the railway station and over Lendal Bridge before turning down Petergate and heading back towards Shambles. It was a route full of tourists and shoppers but was also dotted with men and women of all ages, huddled in sleeping bags or sitting cross-legged in front of handwritten signs, empty coffee cups and upturned caps. Shadow was well aware that some were professional beggars, who travelled in each day from Leeds, Hull and Middlesbrough, looking for easy pickings in a city so popular with wealthy visitors. However, there were others who had become part of the fabric of York. They were as familiar to the other residents as the city walls or the River Ouse.

Byron was one such figure. He had been a permanent resident of The Haven for the last nine months. Previously, however, he'd been one of the city's worst street drinkers and spent countless nights in police cells. A tall man, he was never seen without his Tilley hat and could often be heard loudly giving directions to confused tourists. Most days he sold a newspaper, called *Helping Hand*, in aid of a homeless charity. His usual pitch was outside Marks and Spencer's on Parliament Street, but this afternoon Shadow spotted him next to the ice cream van by the Minster. They nodded to each other in recognition.

"Detective Chief Inspector Shadow, I heard you were looking into what happened to poor little Fay." His voice was deep and booming and betrayed his London roots.

Shadow shook his outstretched hand. "Did you know her well, Byron?"

"Not very. She'd been at The Haven on and off for the last six months or so. She was a nice kid, could be a bit wild, but who of us wasn't at that age?"

Shadow smiled in agreement, although he struggled to remember a time, he had ever done anything that could be considered wild.

"We think the vodka she drank, before she died might have been tampered with," he explained, careful not to use the words poison or cyanide, "so remember to take care should anyone offer you some on the cheap."

Byron ran his hand over the stubble on his chin. "Iffy booze about eh? Well, no need to warn me, Inspector, I'm as clean as a whistle these days. I've even gone vegan."

"Really?" asked Shadow, appalled at the thought of a diet without meat, butter, or cheese. Byron nodded his head, vigorously.

"Best thing I ever did. Luke and Susie inspired me. They grow all their own fruit and veg, and they both look great on it. I feel amazing. You know, like really cleansed." He spoke enthusiastically, with the evangelical zeal of the recently converted, but Shadow remained unconvinced.

"Well good for you, but if you hear of anything about the vodka, let me know."

They shook hands again and Shadow continued on his way.

MAD ALICE WAS a relatively new addition to the streets of York. She seemed to have appeared from nowhere, a few months ago. From her accent, she sounded as though she should be judging a Home Counties gymkhana, not that she made much sense when she did speak. Mostly, she was heard reciting random lines of poetry. For some reason she had made the entrance to Lund's Court her home. It was a snickelway off Petergate and despite the council's best efforts to make it sound more politically correct, it was still known by the locals, as Mad Alice Lane.

The original Mad Alice had been so badly beaten by her husband that she eventually snapped and was hanged for his murder in 1825. Her name had been bestowed on the new resident, who was otherwise anonymous. When Shadow approached her, she was sitting with her legs curled under her on a large, very faded velvet cushion. She was clutching several tattered books to her chest and swaying along to the accordionist, playing further along the street. She seemed so content, he almost didn't want to disturb her.

"Good afternoon, would you like something to eat or drink?" he asked, politely. She pushed her long grey hair away from her face and looked up at the chief inspector. She had very dark eyes and small, delicate, birdlike features. Shadow thought she must have once been quite pretty.

"Oh, how terribly kind, but as you can see this wonderful music is feeding my soul."

Shadow smiled, but privately thought she needed a lot more than music. The woman was a bag of bones. He put his hand in his coat pocket and fished out the card he'd picked up from the reception desk at The Haven. He laid it on the cushion next to her.

"There is a place you could go. Have you tried here?"

"Oh, I mustn't go anywhere. I have to stay exactly where I am," she replied without bothering to look at the card.

Shadow tried again. "The Haven is very nice. Miss Slater and Mr Carrington are good people, who will help you."

She stared up at him and her dark eyes filled with tears, as she slowly started to rock back and forth, then began to whisper. "But one by one we must all file on, through the narrow aisles of pain."

Hurriedly, Shadow decided to change tack. He leant

forward, hoping to make her understand. "If anyone offers you a drink. I mean something alcoholic, especially a bottle of vodka, please don't take it."

Her expression and voice changed instantly, suddenly she became very serious. "Drinking is absolutely forbidden when on duty. It's such a responsibility we have been entrusted with, to care for others," she replied, gripping his arm and earnestly looking him straight in the eye.

Shadow nodded, unsure if he was included in the 'we' or if she had really heard what he'd said. With a sigh, he placed a ten-pound note under the card for The Haven, then waved her goodbye.

SHADOW CONTINUED ON his mission into Kings Square. He squeezed his way through the clapping, cheering crowds of tourists watching the fire-eater who was balancing on a unicycle, until he reached the top of Shambles. Norman the Gnome, as generations of the city's children had called him, was short and squat with a grey beard and a woolly hat he wore in all weathers. He looked much older than his fifty-four years and had been on the streets for most of his adult life. Sounding like a character straight out of a Dickens's novel, he was blatant in his requests for money.

"Any spare change, sir? Any spare change for the home-less? God bless you, sir, God bless you. Any spare change?"

Shadow watched him for a moment. He knew he could keep this verbal stream flowing for at least an hour, or until he'd scraped together enough to make a trip to the off-licence. Most people ignored him, but some stopped to help. He waved away all offers of food or a warm drink, always coming up with some excuse why only cash would do. Today, he was telling them that he needed ten pounds to buy new shoes. Shadow knew this to be nonsense; the Salvation Army had always clothed him.

"Afternoon, Norman, having a good day?"

Norman glanced up but didn't meet Shadow's eye. "Any spare change for the homeless, sir?"

Their paths had crossed countless times over the years. Norman's record was long, but not very illustrious, and full of charges for vagrancy, being drunk and disorderly, and with the occasional outraging public decency thrown in. Shadow rummaged through his pockets for his wallet.

"Look, clear off now and go buy yourself some gin, or rum, or brandy, whatever you want, but not vodka, you hear. Anything but vodka." Shadow held out a twenty-pound note, Norman paused for a split second before snatching it and staggering to his feet. Shadow watched as he hobbled away, calling out once again. "Not vodka, Norman!"

Shadow waited until Norman disappeared around the corner, then turned around to find himself face-to-face with a furious-looking woman. She had blonde, bobbed hair and was immaculately dressed in a bright red suit. Her make-up was perfect and heavily applied, and her well-manicured hands were placed firmly on her hips.

"What on earth do you think you are doing?" she asked, angrily. "You'll only encourage him, giving him money like that. He's an alcoholic, you know."

"I do know. My name is Detective Chief Inspector Shadow…" he began to explain, but the angry woman immediately interrupted him.

"Well it's about time! I've been complaining about him and the others for weeks now. It's all because of that damned soup kitchen. They think they have a right to be here!"

"I'm sorry, er Mrs…?"

"Morrison. Mrs Mandy Morrison. I own the Angelique Boutique." She pointed to the ladies' wear shop behind her on the corner of Shambles. "This is prime tourist season and having the likes of him practically sitting on my doorstep, bothering customers, can ruin a business. I have been on to your lot, the council, everyone to do something and what happens when you do finally arrive? You give him money! I mean…"

Shadow was aware that many of the tourists were finding their argument more entertaining than the fire-eater. One Japanese man had even started to film them.

"Mrs Morrison, I do apologise, but this is a matter for the uniform section. I will ask them to give it their full attention. Good evening."

With that Shadow made his escape, leaving Mrs Morrison still complaining loudly behind him in the street.

HE WAS RELIEVED when he finally returned to the peace and quiet of the river. Shadow's home was a narrow boat, moored on the River Ouse close to Skeldergate Bridge. He had bought the boat, named *Florence*, when he worked down in London for the Metropolitan Police. The alternative had been paying a fortune for a shoebox in the city, or a long commute by tube, which he hated. There was also the fact he could change the view from his window whenever he chose, which appealed to him.

Twenty-five years ago, when he'd transferred back up north, he simply navigated his way home through the network canals and rivers. After two weeks, he had swapped his view of Little Venice for one of Clifford's Tower. *Florence* still had everything he needed. There was a large, comfortable bedroom and a compact bathroom with adequate shower. The open-plan galley and living area were small, but then he almost always ate out and never entertained. He and *Florence* had been through a lot together over the years and he had never wanted to live anywhere else.

AS SOON AS he arrived home that evening, he flicked on his

ancient CD player and poured himself a large glass of Barolo. For once he wasn't hungry. The visit to the mortuary was still causing his stomach to churn. He stuck his nose into the glass of wine and inhaled deeply, hoping the aroma of cherries and anise would banish the stench of formaldehyde that was still lingering in his nostrils. Sinking down on to the sofa, he took a large sip as the opening chords of 'Night and Day' fill the room. He leaned back, closed his eyes and began to consider the day's events.

If Fay had been given the poison and killed intentionally, it must have been pre-planned, but there was no obvious motive. On the other hand, if it was an illegal batch of vodka that had somehow been tampered with and was now contaminated, then surely there would have been more than one casualty. He took another sip of wine and eased off first one shoe, then the other.

Tomorrow they needed to trace the vodka, check if there was any CCTV of Fay, then track down Ryan and Kayleigh. He wondered how quickly the lab would have the results for the vodka. Uniform would do their best to get the message out to the publicans, but the most vulnerable, those on the streets, would be the hardest to find and the least willing to listen. The thought of a mass poisoning in the city filled him with dread and deserved another large mouthful of Barolo.

At that moment, his train of thought was interrupted by a cheerful 'rat-a-tat' on the door. Shadow groaned. Only one person could still sound that upbeat at the end of a busy day.

"Come in, Jimmy. It's open," he called out, reluctantly putting his glass of wine down. The sergeant ducked his head low as he came through the door and down the steps. He needed to continue to stoop as he walked towards the sofa. It was the first time he'd visited his boss at home, but he looked unfazed by being on the boat.

"Sorry to bother you, Chief," he said, not sounding remotely sorry, "but another body's been found."

"Is it Mad Alice?" Shadow asked immediately, without knowing why she should be the first person to spring into his mind. Jimmy looked slightly puzzled but shook his head.

"No, we don't know who it is yet. When I said body, I really meant skeleton. It's in Museum Gardens. Some builders found it when they were working on the Hospitium," he explained.

"For crying out loud, Sergeant! This is York. Whenever someone digs down more than a few inches they find something. The last time they dug the station car park up they found half a Viking army. Call the archaeologists in. It's bound to be the remains of a Roman gladiator or some medieval plague victim."

Shadow picked up his glass again and took another drink while Jimmy shifted uncomfortably from foot to foot.

"The York Historic Foundation were called first, sir. You see they own the Hospitium and insisted they should be notified first if anything unusual was found. They took a look at the skeleton and, well it's definitely one for us, sir."

Shadow cursed under his breath, knocked back the remaining wine and pulled on his shoes.

"I'll be back in a minute," he said, before disappearing towards the bathroom. When he returned, he found Jimmy with several CDs in his hand, peering at his stereo as if it was from another planet.

"You know sir, if you got some speakers you could listen to music through your phone. I could download all these old CDs and more for you. It would take up a lot less space." He retrieved his own mobile phone from his pocket to demonstrate. Shadow looked at it in horror.

"No thank you, Sergeant. If it was up to me, a voice as great as Ella Fitzgerald's would only ever be heard on long-playing records. And a big band certainly doesn't belong on anything as tiny as that thing."

"Maybe you could buy a record player then, Chief. They are popular again. Vinyl's making a comeback."

"I don't need any more clutter collecting dust," declared Shadow, pulling on his old wax jacket. Jimmy frowned as he glanced around the boat. Aside from the vast music collection and a few old copies of the *Yorkshire Post*, there were no personal effects to be seen.

SHADOW LOCKED THE door and the two men stepped on to the towpath. A couple walked by with a golden retriever, and two geese flew over their heads and landed noisily on the river.

"Are you a big music fan, Chief? Do you go to many gigs?" asked Jimmy.

Shadow's brow folded into several deep furrows. He couldn't understand his new sergeant's insistence on trying to make small talk at every opportunity. "No, Sergeant. As far as I'm concerned, all the musical greats are dead. I just have to make do with their recordings."

Jimmy pressed on enthusiastically, despite Shadow hoping he had shut down the conversation.

"So, do you play any instruments yourself, sir? The guitar or the piano maybe?"

"No." Shadow sighed, then chuckled to himself. "As Frank Sinatra used to say, I've got a beat like a cop."

"Yeh? That's great." Jimmy laughed awkwardly, then after a short pause, "Who's Frank Sinatra, Chief?"

CHAPTER THREE

Down 5 (6 letters)
Let the nun go underground

MUSEUM GARDENS WAS a public park in the centre of York. It surrounded the Yorkshire Museum that housed the city's archaeological treasures and gave the park its name. It had one entrance on Museum Street and one on Marygate and ran down to the edge of the River Ouse. It also contained the ruins of St Mary's Abbey and the Hospitium, which had once given shelter to medieval travellers visiting the city, but was now hired out for weddings, christenings and other celebrations. It was a beautiful two-storey timber-framed building in the classic black and white style, with a stone staircase on the outside leading up to a balcony. However, despite its many attractive qualities, its plumbing wasn't quite twenty-first century, hence the current building work.

It was just after dusk when Shadow and Jimmy arrived at the gardens' tall black wrought-iron entrance gates. They were locked to the public, but a uniformed constable let them through. In the distance, they could see the white glow from the floodlights now surrounding the Hospitium. Sophie Newton, the police's other pathologist, was hauling herself out of a freshly dug trench, as the two policemen approached.

"Evening, Chief. Evening, Jimmy," she called out cheerfully, peeling off her latex gloves.

"What have you got for us, Sophie?" asked Shadow, taking the doctor's outstretched hand and helping her climb out. She pointed down to the skeleton occupying the hole.

"Difficult to be accurate until I get her back to the lab, but I'd say she was in her late teens or early twenties and was probably killed between twenty-five and thirty years ago. Richard Stather, he's head of archaeology at the foundation," she continued, gesturing to a dark-haired, bespectacled man with a neatly clipped moustache, talking earnestly to a younger man, "he got here first. I think he's a bit miffed that it's not one for him. He did say the last time he could remember any sort of building work taking place in this area, was when they were improving the boat shed down by the towpath and that was over thirty years ago."

"Any idea how she was killed?" asked Shadow, peering cautiously down into the hole.

"Looks like a trauma, possibly two traumas to the head with a blunt instrument."

"Like a hammer?" asked Jimmy, who was busily making notes.

Sophie shrugged. "Maybe or something bigger—like I

said, I'll know more when I get back to the lab. I'll be in touch tomorrow."

"Okay—thanks, Sophie." Shadow shook her outstretched hand again. Even with the gloves removed, he didn't like to think about what it may have been touching previously. He motioned for Jimmy to follow him and made his way over to the archaeologist, who also looked to be busy making notes.

"Mr Stather, I'm Detective Chief Inspector Shadow. May I ask you a few questions?"

"Of course, of course it's quite the exciting night for you I imagine, but disappointing for us. Oh, and not to be pedantic, Chief Inspector, but it's actually Doctor Stather." He gave a small, self-conscious laugh.

Shadow smiled tightly, as Jimmy hid his face behind his notebook.

"I understand the last time this area saw any excavation work was about thirty years ago?" Shadow continued.

"That's correct, thirty-two years ago to be exact. I've just checked my records. If you look down by the river, you'll see what remains of an old boathouse. It used to belong to St John's School. They used it for their rowing club and wanted to make improvements, add showers and so forth. As the builders started work, it became clear that the boathouse was built on top of what used to be the water gate for the Hospitium. There was a tunnel that led directly to the Hospitium. In those days, we only had a couple of weeks to excavate, before it was bricked up again."

Dr Stather spoke smoothly as if giving a lecture, while Jimmy dutifully took notes. Shadow thought there was something about this doctor that reminded him of Donaldson. He didn't want to prolong their meeting.

"Well thank you, Dr Stather, and I'm sorry your evening has been wasted."

SHADOW AND JIMMY waited for the remains of the victim to be removed, before they also made their way out of the Museum Gardens.

"Tomorrow get on to the main records office at county and ask for the details of any female missing persons from around thirty-two years ago," instructed Shadow as he waved his thanks to the constable, who opened the gate again. "Then get back to the Fay Lawton case. That has to be our priority. If there is a batch of dodgy vodka, we need to make sure nobody else drinks it."

Suddenly Jimmy stopped in his tracks and pointed across the road towards Library Square.

"Look who it is, sir."

Shadow looked over and saw Ryan and Kayleigh sprawled together against the library wall, their rucksacks next to them. Both were well known to the police. They had been in and out of prison for everything from shoplifting to assault. Ryan was a thin, skinhead with arms covered in tattoos. Kayleigh was equally skinny and tattooed with long dark hair, scraped back into a high ponytail.

"What do you want?" she asked aggressively, as Shadow and Jimmy approached.

"To offer our condolences," replied Shadow, easily. "We understand a close friend of Ryan's died last night." Kayleigh scowled.

"What's it got to do with you?" asked Ryan, with a sneer.

"We think the vodka she drank killed her. We'd like to know where she got it from."

"Not us."

"Then who?"

Ryan shrugged his bony shoulders.

"How should we know? We were at Ted's all night."

"Where you argued with Fay?"

"We didn't argue; she just got upset when I said I was back with Kayleigh."

He threw a scrawny arm around his girlfriend, who slumped closer to him with a broken-toothed grin.

"Do you know if she had any money with her when she left?" Shadow persisted.

"She better not have done," snarled Kayleigh. "She said she was skint. Me and Ryan was subbing her all day."

"I see, well thank you for your time."

Shadow and Jimmy turned away, leaving Kayleigh and Ryan sniggering behind them.

"He wasn't exactly heartbroken was he, sir," observed Jimmy, after a few minutes of silence.

"No," sighed Shadow, "but that doesn't necessarily mean he's guilty."

Shadow wished his deputy goodnight and headed back to the river. Several questions bothered him. Why was Dr Stather, who clearly considered himself an important man, still in Museum Gardens long after it had been established that the body was of no archaeological interest? If Fay really didn't have any money then someone must have given her the vodka, but who? And why did Susie keep chickens if she was a vegan?

THE NEXT MORNING, Shadow managed to enjoy his breakfast uninterrupted, and had been at his desk, with his crossword, for half an hour before the Minster bells struck nine. He was on the cusp of completing the next clue, when Jimmy knocked and then put his head round the door.

"I've got news on the vodka, Chief."

"You'd better come in and sit down then," said Shadow, reluctantly folding his newspaper away into the desk drawer. Jimmy quickly slipped into the chair opposite him and began reading from his digital notebook.

"Well it's not cheap stuff. It's a premium brand called Holy Cow and it's distilled on Lindisfarne, you know, Holy

Island, up in Northumberland?" Shadow raised an impatient eyebrow, as Jimmy continued, "I've just been speaking to the owner of the distillery. It's fascinating what they do. They use milk from local cows. You see the curds go to make cheese, but the leftover whey is normally thrown away, so instead…"

Shadow held up his hands in protest. "All right, all right, I don't need a lesson in vodka production. It sounds disgusting."

"Well actually, it's meant to have a smooth vanilla taste," continued Jimmy, then saw the look on Shadow's face, "but the main thing is, it's only produced in seventy-centilitre and five-centilitre bottles. The bottle Fay had was fifty-centilitres and the label was a photocopy stuck on. By the way, forensics said no fingerprints except Fay's."

"Is it sold wholesale or retail?"

"Both, but they just supply one shop in York."

Shadow waited expectantly, his fingers drumming his desk.

"Am I meant to guess, Sergeant?"

"Sorry, Chief." Jimmy brushed his floppy dark fringe out of his eyes, as he searched down the page of his notebook. "It's Bacchus, that posh wine shop on Shambles."

Shadow stood up and retrieved his wax jacket from the back of his chair. "Then let's head to Shambles."

YORK'S OLDEST AND most famous street was packed with tourists as always and the two detectives could only shuffle along behind the crowd. Norman was once again slumped at the top of the street, a stained sleeping bag over his knees despite the warm weather. As Shadow passed the ladies' boutique, a furious tapping on the window caught his attention. He turned to see the equally furious face of Mandy Morrison mouthing and pointing at Norman, then back at Shadow. Shadow inclined his head politely and kept walking.

"Wow, what have you done to upset Mrs Morrison, sir?" asked Jimmy, trying his best not to smile. Shadow scowled.

"We had a slight disagreement last night, over the problem of homelessness in the city. How do you know her?"

"Everyone knows Mrs Morrison—she complains about everything." Jimmy laughed. "The noise from the buskers, the bins not being emptied often enough. When one of the shop windows got smashed, she came down to the station and demanded a twenty-four-hour police presence on Shambles. Didn't you see her in the *Herald* the other night?"

"I make a point of never reading that rag," grunted Shadow. Instead, he always bought the *Yorkshire Post*, particularly since the city's own paper had employed Kevin MacNab, a new, pushy young crime reporter, whom Shadow found particularly irritating.

"Well, there was a picture of her handing a petition in to the council," explained Jimmy. "It said the local traders wanted them to take action against the beggars and cancel the soup kitchen in Kings Square."

"The soup kitchen Susie Slater and Luke Carrington run?"

"Yes, Chief. Remember Susie said it's on every Tuesday and Saturday evening. According to Mrs Morrison it attracts 'undesirables' to the area."

Jimmy paused to allow some Americans to take a group photo.

Shadow turned to him. "Get hold of a copy of that petition. Let's see who else wants to get rid of the homeless."

BACCHUS WAS HOUSED halfway down Shambles, in a building that used to be one of the medieval butchers' shops. It still had the meat hooks outside and the wide wooden benches under the window, that gave the street its name. However, instead of rancid meat and bits of offal, it now sold expensive and rare wines and spirits. Inside, the lighting was soft, the wooden floor and shelves were well polished and classical music played quietly in the background.

Bacchus was owned by Oliver Harrison, who had a neatly trimmed grey beard and wore a multicoloured bow tie with his well-cut navy suit. His charming and welcoming smile barely flickered when he heard who the two men standing in front of him were and what they wanted to talk to him about.

"Holy Cow is one of our best sellers, Chief Inspector," he explained, smoothly. "Here, why don't you and the sergeant have a taste? Just a small one, I know you're on duty." Oliver took a bottle of the vodka from under the counter and splashed a measure into two of the shot glasses neatly lined up on a tray in front of him.

"By the way, you are quite right to say it only comes in seventy-centilitre or five-centilitre bottles."

"Isn't five-centilitres a bit small?" asked Jimmy, cautiously sniffing the shot glass before knocking it back.

"We only sell those bottles in batches of a hundred. People buy them to include in a gift bag, say for a birthday party, a corporate event or wedding favour—that sort of thing," replied Oliver, as he refilled the glass.

"I don't suppose you keep a list of customers who buy Holy Cow?" asked Shadow, frowning at Jimmy, as his own shot glass remained untouched. He wasn't a big fan of spirits.

Oliver laughed easily and shook his head. "I'm sorry, Chief Inspector, no. We sell, on average five bottles a day. Some are to local, regular customers, but most are to tourists. You can see for yourself we get visitors from all over the world." He gestured to the crowds outside. "This morning alone, I have sold to two Chinese gentlemen, one Spanish lady and a French couple. The mini bottles of course are easier, because they need to be ordered in advance, so I can certainly give you a list of those customers."

"Thank you, that would be very helpful. By the way, Mr Harrison, did you sign the petition Mandy Morrison organised, regarding the soup kitchen?"

"No, I didn't," he replied, then hesitated and nervously fiddled with his bow tie. "It was quite a tricky situation actually, Chief Inspector. I don't know if you have met Mandy, but she's not an easy woman to say no to and to be fair, I agree that perhaps having a soup kitchen in such a prominent position doesn't do much to elevate the image of the city." His hand moved from his bow tie to his glasses, which he removed and began to clean. "However, Susie and Luke are two of my oldest friends. Luke was in the year below me at St. John's and Susie was my sister's best friend when we were growing up. I wouldn't like to do anything to upset her. I mean, after all, it is for a good cause isn't it?"

He paused again and frowned. "Actually, Chief Inspector, now I come to think of it, both Mandy and Susie have ordered the five-centilitre bottles of Holy Cow."

"Really? Recently?" asked Shadow.

"In the last couple of months or so. Mandy put them in gift bags for a fashion show she was holding and Susie wanted them for a birthday party she was throwing for Luke's fiftieth. They were supposed to go in the party bags for guests. It caused a bit of a row actually. You see, Luke's gone vegan and when he found out Holy Cow is essentially made from milk, he absolutely hit the roof."

"So, what happened?" asked Jimmy, who had downed

the second shot and was now tapping away furiously at his notebook.

Oliver shrugged. "Susie sorted it. She always does. Luke would be lost without her. The woman is a saint. That's why I couldn't possibly sign that awful petition, Chief Inspector."

THE TWO POLICE officers left Bacchus and took a short walk to their next destination. Ted's Bar stood on Colliergate, which ran parallel to Shambles, but instead of souvenir and luxury gift shops for tourists, it catered for local residents and was home to a hardware store, post office and chemist's shop. Ted's owner's real name was Chris Barton, but he'd taken to dressing as a Teddy Boy when he was a teenager and the name had stuck. Despite the fact the style had not been fashionable for decades, he still maintained the look. His thinning hair was died black and shaped into a large quiff and he wore skinny black jeans and a brightly coloured, oversized jacket.

During the many years he had been proprietor of the bar, he had been in trouble with the police for various offences, from allowing underage drinking, to watering down spirits, but the authorities had never managed to close him down. He and Shadow knew each other well.

"What do you want?" he asked gruffly, when Shadow and Jimmy walked into the bar. It was just after opening time. The place was empty, except for Ted and a tall, thin barmaid. Ted sat in a corner, reading the *York Herald* with his feet up on a table. The barmaid had short, bleached-blonde hair and was busy restocking the shelf behind the bar. The walls were covered in black-and-white photographs of rock-and-roll stars from the 1950s and 60s. Underfoot, the wooden floor was sticky with spilt, stale beer and a jukebox in the corner was playing 'Great Balls of Fire'. Shadow and Jimmy sat down opposite the owner.

"We wanted to talk to you about Fay Lawton," replied Shadow, evenly.

Ted swung his legs down and spread the newspaper open on the table, pointing to the article he had been reading. "It says in here you lot are investigating. What's to investigate?"

Shadow glanced down. The photograph accompanying the article was of Fay smiling in a garden. Shadow thought it could be The Haven garden.

"She was poisoned."

"Not in here she wasn't," Ted shot back, quickly. "Some of your lot have already been on the phone. Giving me a lecture on not buying cheap vodka. Well, you're not pinning any of this on me."

"But Fay was drinking in here the night she died?"

"Yes, and so were plenty of others, but none of them dropped dead. Look, she was in here with Ryan and Kayleigh. They were having quite a session, then there was a row and Fay ran off."

"What did they row about?" Shadow asked, but Ted simply shrugged.

"How should I know? Lover's tiff maybe."

"And the other two?"

"I let them have a bit of a lock-in as they were celebrating. Kayleigh had only got out that morning. I went to bed, but they were drinking 'til the early hours. Isn't that right, Cristina, love?"

"Yes, they passed out at about two o'clock," agreed the blonde girl behind the bar. She was now polishing glasses and spoke with a heavy Eastern European accent. "That is when I went to bed. Ted was already asleep upstairs. I woke them up when I came down in the morning and they left."

Ted leaned back in his chair and grinned at the two policemen.

"Who would have thought it, Shadow? I'd turn out to be the Good Samaritan in all this. Giving two pissed-up vagrants a bed for the night, when goody two shoes Slater and Carrington turned away that poor young girl! She should have come back here—she might still be alive."

"Fay was a good girl," said Cristina suddenly from the other side of the bar, as if this was the final word on the matter.

The two policemen got up to leave. When they had almost reached the door, Jimmy turned back. "If they were all homeless, how could they afford to be drinking here all night?"

Ted had already returned to his newspaper and didn't bother to lower it when he replied, "I'm not their bank manager, lad. As long as they can pay, what do I care?"

Shadow and Jimmy both blinked as they stepped out from the dingy bar into the bright sunshine.

"Sorry, Chief, it was a stupid question to ask," Jimmy said, looking embarrassed.

In an unusually understanding gesture, Shadow patted him on the back. "Not really. I have plenty of stupid questions of my own that he wouldn't have answered either. I'm sure he knows what the argument between Fay and Ryan was about and I'd also like to know the real reason he let Ryan and Kayleigh sleep here that night?"

"You don't see Ted as a Good Samaritan, then, sir?"

"If he's the Good Samaritan, then I'm St Peter, Sergeant."

Suddenly there was a crash behind them. They turned to see Cristina tipping a box full of bottles into the recycling bin in the alleyway next to the bar. When she saw she was being observed, she tossed her head defiantly and stalked back inside. Shadow and Jimmy watched her go.

"Even if Ryan and Kayleigh really did spend the whole night here, one or both of them could easily have slipped out, found Fay and given her the vodka," Jimmy suggested.

Shadow shook his head.

"Ryan might be a nasty piece of work, but if he really wanted to get rid of Fay, I don't see him going to all the trouble of buying an expensive bottle of vodka, getting hold of some cyanide and then pouring the whole lot into another bottle. No, Ryan's more the type to smash the bottle over her head."

"Look over there, sir; that might help."

Shadow turned to look where Jimmy was pointing across the street to the post office. Above the door was a CCTV camera facing Ted's Bar.

"Go and see if it's recorded anything. And when you are done there, see if there are any cameras on Goodramgate near where Fay was found. I think it's time I had a chat with Luke Carrington. Ted made a point of mentioning his name to us. If I know Ted, he wouldn't have done without a reason."

AS SHADOW LEFT Jimmy, he called The Haven, and Jess told him that both Susie and Luke were at home. Since they had turned the Carrington house into The Haven, Susie and Luke now lived in an apartment in Granary Court, off St Andrewgate. Fortunately, it was merely a short walk from Kings Square. He was about to make his way there when someone tapped him sharply on the shoulder. He turned around to see the unwelcome sight of a shock of bright ginger hair and Kevin MacNab's freckled face grinning at him.

"Good morning, Chief Inspector Shadow. Would you like to comment on your investigation into the death of Fay Lawton? I know the *Herald* readers would be keen to hear from the officer in charge."

"Really? Even though you've already printed your story in today's edition?"

"I did try calling your office, but they told me you were unavailable."

"I still am," replied Shadow in irritation, as he turned on his heel and strode away. It was typical of MacNab to get under his feet, rather than talk to the press officer at county headquarters, like everyone else.

A few moments later, he was at Granary Court. From the outside, it was a large, rather dull, modern red-brick building standing where an old Victorian flour mill had once been. There was a main door that accessed six flats, but the penthouse, where Susie and Luke lived, had its own door on the left. He was about to press the button for the intercom, when the door was flung open and Susie Slater almost knocked him over. She was dressed in black and pink Lycra shorts and cropped top, with her hair in a high ponytail.

"Oh, Chief Inspector, I'm so sorry, I was just on my way out for a run."

"That's quite all right, Miss Slater," Shadow replied, managing to regain his balance, "I actually wanted to speak to Mr Carrington."

"Would you mind showing yourself up? I'm afraid the

lift's on the blink, but the door to the flat is open. Luke might not hear you—he's meditating on the balcony."

Without waiting for Shadow to reply, she sprinted off towards Kings Square, her ponytail swinging behind her. Shadow watched her go then turned and headed up the stairs. By the time he had reached the top of the third flight, he felt like he'd run a marathon. He paused for a moment to catch his breath, relieved nobody was there to see him. As Susie had said, the door to the penthouse was open.

Once he was breathing normally again, Shadow stepped inside, to a large open-plan room, with high ceilings. It combined a living, dining and kitchen area. The walls were painted white and the pale wooden floors were highly polished. The huge sofas were also white, while the furniture was all glass and gleaming chrome. One wall was covered in framed gold discs and album covers from Susie's previous career. On another, hung vast abstract canvases of distorted faces. It was difficult to tell if they were male or female. Shadow thought they were hideous.

He had wondered why Susie and Luke had chosen to live in such a plain building, having been used to the beautiful Georgian house, but now he could see why. The whole of one side of the room was glass and through it was the most perfect view of the Minster. A deep balcony ran along the length of the room. It was covered in greenery and there was a glass structure at the far end. Sitting out there cross-legged, amongst the many plants in pots and tubs, was a man wearing a T-shirt and shorts.

"Mr Carrington," Shadow called out. There was no response. Shadow moved closer, gave a loud cough and tried again. The sliding glass door was wide open. Although the man had his back to him, Shadow was sure he must be able to hear him. He stepped back from the window. Clearly Mr Carrington was not going to be disturbed.

He wandered over to the kitchen area. There were various top-of-the-range gadgets, some of which looked as though they had been designed by NASA, but what really caught his attention was the large cork pin board next to the fridge. It was the only thing in the penthouse that wasn't minimalistic or carefully designed. Instead it was covered in takeaway menus, phone numbers for taxi firms and photographs, all randomly arranged and held in place by multicoloured pins.

The photos had been taken at different times in Luke and Susie's life together. There was one of them both grinning as they sat in a canoe, with a tropical forest as a backdrop. Another was of the two of them in evening dress, standing on a red carpet, at what Shadow assumed was an awards ceremony. One, which must have been taken when they were teenagers, showed them with another boy and girl. It looked like they were in Museum Gardens. As Shadow peered more closely, he realised the other boy was a much younger, clean-shaven Oliver Harrison. He had no idea who the other girl was, but with her dark curls and big brown eyes, she was exceptionally beautiful, and Luke Carrington had his arms firmly wrapped round her waist.

In a more recent snap, Luke and Byron were both giving a thumbs up for the camera. The image next to it made Shadow stare more closely. Standing in what he thought was The Haven garden, smiling for the camera as she sat next to Susie, was Fay Lawton. The image he had in his head was of her pale, damaged and lifeless, yet here she was staring back at him, young, happy and full of life. He was also fairly certain it was the same photograph MacNab had used for his article in the *Herald*.

"Ah, Chief Inspector Shadow, I presume."

Shadow spun round, startled; he'd almost forgotten why he was there. Luke was standing behind him, looking very relaxed to find a strange man in his kitchen.

"They phoned from The Haven to say you might call in," he explained. "Forgive me, but I can't be disturbed when I'm meditating. Can I get you a drink?"

Luke opened the fridge door and brought out a bottle containing a thick, dark green liquid. Shadow thought it looked like bottled seaweed.

"No thank you," he replied, politely.

As Luke knocked back the suspicious liquid, Shadow had a chance to take a proper look at him. He was tall, slim, toned and tanned. His dark hair was streaked with grey and he wore it long and tied back in a ponytail.

"Have you and Miss Slater lived here long?" Shadow

asked.

"Since we turned my folks' old place into The Haven. Susie found it. She's great at that kind of thing. I told her I needed plenty of light so I could paint and voila! What could be more perfect than this place? As soon as I walked in, I felt it had a really positive, creative energy," Luke explained, waving his arm around airily.

Shadow attempted to smile as he realised, with horror that Luke Carrington might well be responsible for the monstrosities hanging on the wall.

"How long have the two of you been together?"

"Since we were kids. My dad was her manager back when she was a singer. I was meant to go to uni, but I went a bit wild after sixth form. Susie was fantastic, she really helped me find my focus again. We spent a lot of time travelling in Thailand and South America, you know, living with some local tribes. I really grew as a person, made me realise how unimportant material things are."

Shadow nodded sagely, while taking in the designer watch on Luke's wrist and the expensive coffee machine behind him.

"Did you become a vegan while you were travelling?"

Luke stared into the distance, as if he was giving the question very serious consideration. "I would say mentally yes, but physically it was more like a year ago. It was a long process to realise what is better for my body is also better for the planet."

"And Miss Slater feels the same?"

"Yeh man, Susie has been so amazing. She grows organic fruit and vegetables in the garden at The Haven and out there on the balcony, she's practically recreated the rainforest."

He gestured to where he'd been sitting outside and Shadow reasoned the glass structure must be a greenhouse. The last thing Shadow wanted was a lecture on the benefits of a vegan life, so he briskly moved on.

"I'm actually here to ask you about Fay Lawton."

"Oh man, what a tragedy! I've felt so traumatised since I heard, you know, real pain right here." Luke thumped his chest dramatically with his fist. "I haven't been able to even pick up my brushes. The only solace has been my music." He turned towards a guitar propped up against one of the sofas.

"You're a musician as well as an artist?" asked Shadow, trying to keep the sarcasm out of his voice.

"I have been truly blessed."

"A left-handed player, I see."

"All the greats are: Hendrix, McCartney, Cobain." Luke laughed self-consciously and walked over to the window. He beckoned Shadow to follow him. Shadow did so reluctantly. Luke pointed solemnly out towards the Minster. "That's where my musical awakening began. As a boy, I was one of the choristers at the Minster. Emma, Susie and I were all recruited at the same time. That's when the unbreakable bond was formed."

"Who's Emma?" asked Shadow. Luke pulled his phone out of his pocket and showed his screen saver to Shadow. It was the same photo he'd just seen on the pin board of Luke, Susie, Oliver and the mystery girl.

"Emma Harrison. Another young life taken too soon." He sighed deeply and briefly stroked the screen. "That's what I'm thinking of calling my next song: 'Taken Too Soon.'"

Shadow resisted the urge to roll his eyes. "Unfortunately, there is more bad news. We believe Fay's death was not an accident. There was poison in the vodka she drank."

Luke shook his head as he slipped the phone back into his pocket. "Wow that's crazy, man. So, you think she killed herself. I know she was upset about Ryan and she did have history of self-harming, but wow." He stepped back from the window and sank down on to one of the sofas.

"Were you at The Haven the night Fay died?"

"No, I was here. Asleep. Dead to the world. Susie spoke to her. She said she was in a state. Fay saw Susie as a kind of maternal figure; she relied on her a lot. Susie felt really bad about not letting her stay, but I told her, we have a policy, 'It's a no to the three Ds – drink, drugs and dogs.'"

"No exceptions? Not even for a young, vulnerable girl?"

Luke shook his head solemnly. "It wouldn't be fair to the other residents."

"I see, and you can't think of anyone who might want to harm Fay?"

"No way, man, she was a sweet kid, just a bit messed up. Don't worry though, Chief Inspector, if someone did kill Fay, karma will take care of it."

"Karma, good, well that's a relief. It should make our job a lot easier."

Shadow couldn't take anymore. He quickly said goodbye and left, shaking his head as he made his way back down the stairs. Oliver Harrison called Susie Slater a saint earlier, well she was either that or mad to put up with Luke Carrington.

As he stepped out on to St Andrewgate, he found Jimmy waiting for him.

"How did it go, sir?"

"Sadly, we can't arrest someone just for being a prat. How about you? Anything on the CCTV?"

"Yes and no, Chief," Jimmy began. Shadow scowled at him, so he hurried on. "I mean no, Ryan and Kayleigh definitely didn't leave Ted's that night. I rewound the tape to see Fay leave on her own, at 10.40pm and then I went back further, to see what time the three of them arrived and if anyone else was with them. So, they arrived about 2pm and it was just them."

"Is this going anywhere, Sergeant?" sighed Shadow impatiently.

"I'm getting there, sir. At 5.30pm Ross Jones walked into Ted's. A few minutes later he left with Fay and then after about ten minutes she returned alone."

"Ross the street cleaner? Didn't he say he hadn't seen Fay

for years?"

"Yes, sir."

"Well you had better go and speak to him again and see if there is anything he would like to add to his statement. Make sure he knows that obstructing a police officer is a serious offence. When you are done with him, don't forget to see if you can get any CCTV for Goodramgate. I'm going to head back to the station for a while. There are a couple of things I want to check."

Shadow turned briskly on his heel, only to find Jimmy still by his side, tapping away on his mobile phone.

"I'll walk with you, Chief. By the way, I got the council to email me a copy of Mrs Morrison's petition and there are a couple of interesting names on there. Ted and Dr Richard Stather both signed."

Shadow raised an eyebrow.

"So, Ted isn't always so understanding when it comes to the homeless. What's it got to do with Stather?"

"His office is above the Angelique Boutique and he's been quite vocal about how the soup kitchen is, in his words 'lowering the tone.' By the way, sir, there's something else about Stather. Last night he said the Museum Gardens were dug up thirty-two years ago because St John's were renovating the boathouse. So, while I was waiting for you, I phoned the school bursar to see if they had the details of the contractors they used in case you wanted to speak to them. Unfortunately, the bursar was out, so I actually spoke to his secretary, and she's worked there over forty years."

Shadow groaned loudly, so Jimmy hurried on.

"And she said no work was ever carried out on the boat-house. Instead of renovating the old one, they built a new one on the edge of the school playing fields thirty years ago."

"That's odd. Stather seemed very sure." Shadow frowned, as he thought in silence for a few minutes. Finally, he muttered, grudgingly, "Good work, Jimmy."

Jimmy grinned but continued rapidly tapping the small screen.

"What are you doing now?" asked Shadow in exasperation. "It's a miracle you don't walk into a lamppost!"

"Sorry, sir, I'm using an app to give me directions to Ross's address."

"In my day, you'd be expected to know these streets like the back of your hand," Shadow grumbled.

The two men had now reached Low Ousegate. As they walked by All Saints, Shadow noticed Jake and Missy sitting on one of the benches in the small garden behind the church. The two police officers stepped over the low brick wall to join them. Missy immediately jumped down and began barking loudly. Shadow ignored her.

"It turns out you were right about Fay. It wasn't an overdose; she was poisoned."

Jake barely looked up from rolling his next cigarette. "Yeh, what sort of poison?"

"Cyanide."

"Nasty stuff—it nearly got Missy once. She'd been eating cherries. PDSA had to pump her stomach."

"I don't suppose you can think of anyone who might want to harm Fay?"

Jake inhaled deeply from his now lit cigarette and shook his head. "I think you're barking up the wrong tree. I reckon it was all a mistake."

Shadow took the seat recently vacated by the noisy spaniel. "How do you mean?"

"I bet Fay nicked that bottle from The Haven and if there was poison in it—well it was meant for someone else. My money would be on Mother bloody Teresa."

"You mean Miss Slater? Do I take it you're not a fan of hers?"

"Not just me. Missy doesn't like her either and dogs are excellent judges of character."

Shadow turned to see the now quiet Missy, on her back, wagging her tail furiously as Jimmy tickled her tummy.

"Any particular reason for your dislike?"

Jake flicked some ash away dismissively. "Too bloody good to be true."

"So, you don't use the soup kitchen or The Haven?"

"No way! They don't let dogs in, say they are the same as booze and drugs. That's discrimination that is."

BACK AT HIS desk in the station, having finally jettisoned Jimmy, Shadow wondered if Jake could be right. What if the cyanide had been meant for someone else? He knew Susie had purchased Holy Cow, but not used it for the birthday party. Could someone have poisoned it in the hope of targeting Susie or Luke? Is that why it was in a fifty-centilitre bottle? Then, there was Mandy Morrison, who had also bought Holy Cow from Oliver. Surely it was too big a leap to go from complaining about the homeless to poisoning one of them.

In front of him were two folders. One contained a pile of press cuttings about Susie Slater and the other, the old case notes regarding the disappearance of Emma Harrison.

"You know, all this stuff could be put on a computer and emailed to you, sir," the newly recruited constable, who staggered in with the heavy files, had suggested. "It would save time and paper."

"But possibly not your job, Constable," growled Shadow, sending the young man scurrying out of the office. Although he admitted to being a technophobe, Shadow also thought there was a lot to be gained from being able to hold the original case notes in your hand. Seeing notes or annotations the investigating officers had made was often invaluable when he was reviewing an old case.

He opened Emma's folder first. A photograph of the beautiful, young girl smiled up at him. She was wearing the uniform for York Ladies' College, a school that had stood on

Petergate, but had been closed for many years now. He began reading the notes. Emma hadn't just been a pupil there, she had been the star pupil. Head girl, captain of the tennis and hockey teams, lead violin in the orchestra and on her way, everyone thought to Oxford University. She was the daughter of Anne and Philip, who had opened Bacchus shortly after they married. Oliver was her only sibling, older by one year.

It was early one Saturday morning in June, when she disappeared. She and Susie, who both represented the school at rowing, had been training on the river. York Ladies' College didn't have a boathouse of their own, so they used the one in Museum Gardens, belonging to St John's School. According to Susie's statement, they had finished training, she had gone to change, but Emma didn't follow her. After a few minutes, she heard a loud splash. When she ran outside to look, there was no sign of Emma. She assumed her friend had fallen in the river, so she raised the alarm.

As both girls were under eighteen, there should have been a member of staff with them, in this case, a young trainee teacher called Ruth Brooke. It seems she had wandered off into the gardens while the girls were on the river. The officer making the notes suspected she had gone to meet a man, but this had never been confirmed. The statement from Miss Brooke said she had gone to read in the shade of a nearby tree. She too had heard a splash and when she arrived at the river Susie was in the water looking for her friend.

Dive teams were called in and the riverbed dredged, but Emma's body was never found. It was noted that the current on the river was very strong in that area. Susie had indeed jumped into the river before the police arrived. She had got into difficulties herself and had to be hauled out by onlookers.

Opening Susie's file was like stepping into another world. Looking at the many photos of her with professionally styled hair and make-up, it was hard to imagine she had been a schoolgirl only a few months before. When she took part in and eventually won the TV talent show, she claimed she was competing in memory of Emma, her best friend. It seemed the public was touched by the story, but there was an element of sniping from other contestants that she got 'the sympathy vote.'

Most of the other articles covered the release of a new single or review of a concert. More recent cuttings from the local press covered the opening of The Haven. It seemed that while many in the city applauded what they were doing, some of their neighbours were less than impressed to have 'down-and-outs' on their doorstep. It seemed the soup kitchen wasn't the first time Susie and Luke had ruffled the locals' feathers. One piece that did catch Shadow's attention was from a national tabloid written towards the end of Susie's career. "*Star's Search for US Fame Ended By Drugs Shame*" was the title.

"UK starlet Susie Slater, who rose to fame after winning

'Star Search,' had big plans to conquer America, but today those hopes and dreams have been cruelly dashed. Her childhood sweetheart, Luke Carrington, also the son of her manager Den Carrington, has been refused a visa, due to a previous drug conviction. Devastated, Susie refuses to leave behind the love of her life. For Susie, like the title of her smash hit single, it really does seem that 'Love Leads the Way.'"

Shadow removed his glasses and rubbed his tired eyes. Closing both files, he felt reading them had created more questions than answers.

CHAPTER FOUR

Across 9 (4 letters)
Amore—that romance isn't in English

S HADOW LEFT THE office, and as it was a Tuesday, he decided to make his way back to Kings Square, where the soup kitchen was to be held. It had been unseasonably warm all week and his head was crammed with thoughts about Fay and Emma. Rather than taking the direct route, he opted to wander through the city first. Experience taught him this was the best way to clear his mind.

The locals had clearly been caught unawares by the mini heatwave. Girls strolled by in summer dresses exposing stark white legs and shoulders. Street vendors had hastily organised ice cream carts and were now doing a roaring trade.

As he crossed Lendal Bridge, Shadow glanced down and saw something that stopped him in his tracks. On the path below, by the river and along the edge of Museum Gardens, was the unmistakable figure of Mad Alice talking animatedly to Dr Stather. Shadow watched them. Alice was rapidly flapping her hands as she spoke. Stather seemed to be trying to calm her down, but she was clearly upset. Suddenly, she turned and quickly walked away. Shadow waited to see if Stather would follow her, but after a few seconds he too turned away and began walking towards the steps up to the bridge. Shadow had no wish to speak with the doctor again, so he put his head down and hurried on across the river.

BY 5.30PM, IT was still warm, but dark clouds were beginning to gather menacingly in the distance behind the Minster. Kings Square, however, was a hive of activity. A small army of volunteers wearing 'The Haven' T-shirts were setting up trestle tables and an awning, in case the threatening rain arrived early. Ryan and Kayleigh appeared with a couple of others. All four were swigging from cans of strong lager. Susie was unloading crates filled with plastic cutlery and crockery from the back of an estate car, while Luke leant against it and chatted to Byron and Kevin MacNab, of all people.

Shadow frowned. The last thing he needed was the journalist interfering this evening. Just then Kevin shook Luke's hand and left with a cheery wave. Shadow was fairly confident he now knew who had given Kevin the photo of Fay. His eyes followed the journalist as he approached Ryan and Kayleigh's group, then very quickly hurried away again. Judging by the jeering and hand gestures directed at him, they weren't keen on talking to the press either.

Shadow continued to watch the scene in front of him unfold, from his table at the first-floor window of The Duke of York. He sipped a large glass of well-chilled Grillo. In one corner of the square, Mandy Morrison was bossily instructing a young, nervous-looking assistant as they put the metal security grids on the boutique windows. She then made an exaggerated show of attaching padlocks, as Norman shuffled past.

Various other figures, clutching grubby rolled-up blankets and overflowing carrier bags, began to arrive. Shadow did a quick tally. There must be at least twenty people waiting to be fed: some he recognised, some were strangers. A few confused Chinese tourists even joined the back of the line. He strained his eyes, but there was no sign of Mad Alice anywhere.

"Hi, Chief, mind if I join you?" Shadow jumped, almost spilling his wine, and looked up to see Sophie smiling down at him.

"What are you doing here?" he asked, pulling a chair out for her.

"Jimmy said to meet you here. I've got the results for the body we found last night."

"How did he know I was here?" Shadow frowned. He hadn't seen or spoken to Jimmy since they left Jake and Missy. It crossed his mind that Jimmy could have accessed the CCTV screens to track him. The thought made him feel very uncomfortable. At that moment, Jimmy himself appeared. Shadow stood up with a sigh, resigned to the fact his quiet drink was now over.

"So, what are you both drinking?" he asked, grudgingly.

"Just a mineral water, please, sir," replied Jimmy, slipping into the seat next to Sophie.

"Well, I'm off duty, so a pint of cider for me please," said the doctor with a grin.

Shadow made his way downstairs to the bar. Maybe he was old-fashioned, but he didn't feel at all happy about ordering a pint for a woman.

He returned to the table a few moments later, carrying a tray holding the water and two half-pint glasses of cider.

Jimmy and Sophie had their heads together, talking intensely, but stopped abruptly as soon as they saw him.

"Sorry they'd run out of pint glasses," he said, as he put the tray on the table. Sophie gave him a sceptical look, as he placed the two glasses in front of her but she didn't complain.

"What have you two been plotting?" Shadow asked as he sat back down. Jimmy turned slightly pink, but Sophie answered smoothly.

"We were just chatting about mobile phones, Chief."

"As far as I'm concerned, they are the work of the devil," Shadow declared. "We managed perfectly well without them before."

"Oh, I don't know," replied Sophie. "I'd be lost without mine and they are pretty handy for keeping track of people."

Jimmy, who had been quietly sipping his water, suddenly burst into a coughing fit. Shadow thumped him on the back several times.

"Only you could choke on water!" he said unsympathetically.

"Are you okay, Jimmy?" asked Sophie.

"Fine thanks," replied Jimmy, giving her a weak smile.

Shadow turned his attention back to Sophie. "So, what can you tell us about the body?" he asked.

Sophie took a gulp of cider before she began. "I'm really just confirming what I told you last night. The victim was aged between sixteen and twenty and she was killed by a blow to the head. Going on the conditions in the tunnel, I would put her death at between thirty and thirty-three years ago. So, assuming the info from Mr Stather is correct, thirty-two years ago sounds about right."

"I think you'll find that's Dr Stather," said Jimmy with a smile.

Sophie snorted into her drink. "Yeh, everybody wants to be called doctor, until they are on a plane with a guy having a heart attack, then they are nowhere to be seen."

Jimmy laughed, but Shadow shuddered. He had a horrible feeling that he'd likely be the one having a heart attack on a plane with only Stather or, worse, Donaldson in attendance. He took a large sip of wine as Jimmy continued.

"Actually, there is some doubt over what Stather said. But I've checked the records at county and there were three females of the right age, reported missing between thirty and thirty-five years ago." He retrieved his notebook from his pocket and scrolled through. "Sheila Jones, a young homeless girl last seen near Skeldergate Bridge. Jan Rennison, a student with a history of mental health issues, absconded from Bootham Hospital and…"

"Emma Harrison. Seventeen years old. Presumed dead, after falling into the river by Museum Gardens, thirty-two years ago," Shadow interrupted.

Jimmy stared at him. "How did you know, sir?"

"I spent the afternoon reading about the life and times of Susie Slater and Emma Harrison. They were best friends. Emma was Oliver Harrison's sister and Luke Carrington was her boyfriend. It seems the four of them were very close when they were teenagers."

Jimmy slumped back in his chair, looking crestfallen, but Shadow was more concerned to see Sophie had already knocked back her first half.

"Any chance she could have drowned and then been placed in the tunnel, Sophie? Could she have got the head injuries falling into the river?"

Sophie shook her head.

"I don't think so, although it is difficult to be accurate because the tunnel has been flooded so many times over the years. There were two injuries to the skull. At the back, something large and flat—I'm talking at least ten by fifteen centimetres—caused a fracture. It would have been enough to knock her out, but not kill her. Then to the front, a flat circular blunt instrument—about five centimetres in diameter—delivered the blow that killed her, instantly I would say. I certainly don't think they were accidental injuries. Now I have a name, I'll check the dental records and confirm her identity, so you can speak to the next of kin. Thanks for the drink. Have a good night!"

With that, she downed the second half and left.

"Crikey, she could put a rugby team to shame!" Shadow muttered. "Go on then, what else have you written down in that wretched digital notebook of yours today?"

Jimmy took a sip of water then cleared his throat.

"When I left you, I went to visit Ross. As soon as I told him that we knew he had lied, the poor kid burst into tears. He told me he'd seen Fay, for the first time in years, about a week ago. She was with a group who were smoking joints by the War Memorial, although she wasn't smoking herself. Now, Ross had heard cannabis might help relieve his grandad's symptoms, remember I said he had MS, but he didn't know where to get hold of any. He approached Fay when she was on her own and she said she could get him a supply and they arranged to meet at Ted's. That's when we caught them on the CCTV."

"How much money changed hands?"

"Fifty."

Shadow let out a low whistle. "That explains how they could afford to celebrate Kayleigh's release."

"Yes, but Kayleigh said Fay didn't have any money so I thought maybe Ted could be behind it. He's got a conviction for supplying and it would explain why he was happy to let Kayleigh and Ryan stay the night."

"Maybe." Shadow was thoughtful as he sipped his wine. "By the way, did it work?"

"Sir?"

"The cannabis? Did it relieve Grandad's symptoms?"

"Oh yes, huge improvement."

"Anything else?"

"I checked the council's CCTV for the night Fay died. It shows her arriving on Goodramgate with a sleeping bag under her arm at 11.15pm, but there's a bit of a blind spot at the entrance to Bedern, where she was found. A few drunks stagger out of the Cross Keys not long after closing time and at about 11.30pm, three members of staff leave Catania's. I checked and none of them spoke to her. That's it, until Jake and Missy appear."

"Did Fay have the vodka with her, when she arrived?"

"Not unless it was rolled up in the sleeping bag, sir."

"And nobody approaches her at all?"

"No, you can only really see the edge of her sleeping bag, but nobody goes anywhere near her. Oh, the one interesting thing I did notice was Oliver Harrison, earlier in the evening. As he crossed over from Kings Square, he stopped to give some cash to Norman the Gnome, not sure how much, but definitely a note."

"Well, I hope, for his sake, Mandy Morrison didn't see him."

Shadow was about to ask if anyone else of interest had shown up on the CCTV, when they were suddenly interrupted by a commotion from down in the square. Ryan, Kayleigh and their associates, had been knocking back cans of lager and becoming steadily rowdier. Mandy, accompanied by a heavily built, bald man, was now loudly informing them that drinking in the street was not allowed. Kayleigh began screaming and swearing in response. Luke stepped in to try and calm things down, but nobody seemed to be paying him any attention. Susie and the other volunteers continued to serve the hungry queue.

"I suppose we'd better get down there. Get uniform round too." Shadow reluctantly drained his glass, as Jimmy took out his phone.

WHEN THEY STEPPED out into the square, they walked straight into the path of Norman, who was shuffling by, a sleeping bag stuffed under his arm.

"You all right there, Norman? Had a good supper?" asked Shadow.

Before Norman could answer, Susie shouted from across the square. "No dawdling, Norman, get yourself somewhere undercover before the rain comes, like I told you." She waved a rubber gloved hand at the two policemen.

Norman looked up at Shadow with his bloodshot eyes. "She's an angel! An angel from heaven," he declared before continuing on his way, narrowly avoiding the two police cars that had just sped into the square.

"Best see if uniform need your assistance, Sergeant," said Shadow, nodding in their direction.

As Jimmy jogged over to the group causing the disturbance, Shadow located Byron perched on the edge of what had once been the graveyard, for the square's long-demolished church. He was tucking into what looked suspiciously like treacle sponge.

"That doesn't look very vegan," commented Shadow.

"Ah, but it totally is," replied Byron, cheerfully waving his plastic fork at the chief inspector. "It's cassava heavy cake, one of Susie's specialities. It's amazing what they can do. Luke's main course was a mean three bean curry. You should try some, Chief Inspector."

Shadow shook his head. He could think of little worse. There was a loud uproar from the drinkers across the square and Jimmy jogged back across.

"Problem?" asked Shadow.

"Kayleigh's being taken away. She's broken the terms of her release, being drunk and disorderly. It wasn't a popular decision with everyone. Ryan spat at one of the officers, so they've arrested him too."

"Charming," grunted Shadow.

"Ah, the demon drink strikes again," sighed Bryon, as he forked up the last mouthful of cake. The three of them watched as Mandy Morrison and her companion applauded, while Ryan continued to shout and curse at the arresting officers.

"Who's the muscle with Mrs Morrison?" asked Shadow.

"That's Eric Morrison, her husband, Chief. He owned a taxi business in Malton and Scarborough, but now he's operating here in York. According to one of the uniform guys, who used to work over on the coast, he's a nasty piece of work. He's been inside for assault. He didn't take too kindly to some Polish guys setting up a rival taxi firm on his patch, so he and a few of his drivers went around and beat up the owner. Gave him a broken nose, two broken fingers and three cracked ribs."

"He sounds even more amiable than his wife," muttered Shadow. "Come on, Sergeant, there's something else I want to check."

They said goodbye to Byron and returned Susie's rubber-gloved wave. Having finished feeding the hungry line, she was now busy clearing away the plates and pans. The police cars had left and the last of the drinkers were now staggering away.

"Well better late than never. It's about time you lot did something useful," Mandy shouted out to them, as they walked across the square.

"As ever we aim to please, Mrs Morrison," replied Shadow, politely.

"Pity you didn't arrest the lot of them. Causing a disturbance like that when some of us taxpayers are trying to run a business. There's a law that says you can't drink in the street here," Mr Morrison joined in, pointing to the notice attached to a lamppost.

Shadow paused and turned towards the couple. "You are quite right, sir, and speaking of alcoholic beverages, I understand Mrs Morrison purchased one hundred miniature bottles of Holy Cow vodka for a fashion show early this year?"

Mandy and her husband exchanged a puzzled glance, before Eric puffed out his chest.

"So, what if we did? What's that got to do with anything?" he asked, defensively.

"The young homeless girl, who was found dead not far from here, was killed by a contaminated bottle of that particular brand of vodka."

Shadow thought Mandy appeared to pale beneath her thick make-up.

Eric turned to Shadow and pointed a stubby finger at him. "You should be ashamed of yourself, accusing innocent law-abiding citizens like us, when you let scum like those vagrants stay out on the streets. The city would be better off if you got rid of the lot of them. They are nothing but vermin. If I had my way, they'd all be gone." Eric's face was rapidly gaining the colour his wife's had lost.

"We aren't accusing anyone of anything, Mr Morrison, but we'll be in touch about the vodka. Have a good evening, sir." Shadow smiled pleasantly, then he and Jimmy continued across the square. Beneath a tree, on the bench recently vacated by Ryan and Kayleigh, they passed Luke, a rolled-up cigarette in his hand and his guitar by his side.

"Wow, man, those two really need to chill." He sighed, shaking his head and blowing a couple of smoke rings that floated high into the air.

"Luke Carrington, Chief?" asked Jimmy, under his breath.

Shadow gave a slight smile. "How did you guess?"

THE TWO DETECTIVES walked along Petergate, towards a large and imposing brick building. It had once been York Ladies' College. Now on the ground floor, it was an Italian restaurant, La Scuola Femminile, while the upper floors had been converted into luxury apartments. Mad Alice had returned to her usual spot, sitting opposite the restaurant's entrance. Shadow and Jimmy paused to speak with her. The last time Shadow had met her she had seemed quite coherent. However, this evening she was rocking gently back and forth, as she quietly recited poetry to herself. Shadow bent down to hear what she was saying.

"Rough winds do shake the darling buds of May, and

summer's lease hath all too short a date."

"Yes, that's right," agreed Shadow, evenly, "there's a storm brewing. Best get yourself undercover." He pointed to the alleyway behind her, but she didn't seem to hear him and just continued to smile and sway. Shadow stood up and left her in peace, wondering if it was her earlier encounter with Stather, that had upset her.

AS THEY STEPPED through the doors of La Scuola Femminile, Shadow was greeted warmly by Francesco, the owner.

"How good to see you, my friend! We usually see you on Fridays only. I have a table right here for you."

He led the two men through to the dining room and to a window table for two, looking out over Petergate.

"I thought we were here for work, Chief?" whispered Jimmy, uncomfortably.

"There's no rule that says we can't eat and work at the same time," replied Shadow as he briefly glanced through the menu.

"I'm not hungry, sir—I had a burger on the way over."

Shadow tutted disapprovingly and turned to the hovering Francesco. "A mineral water for him please, Francesco, and I'll have a large glass of Grillo. To eat make it the *gamberoni mari e monti* followed by the *branzino zafferano*."

"Excellent choice!" exclaimed the Italian, before disappearing into the kitchen.

"I didn't know you could speak Italian, sir," said Jimmy.

"I'm afraid that's only one of many things you don't know, Sergeant Chang. For example, you also didn't know that the room we now sit in was once the school hall, where a young Emma Harrison and Susie Slater would have attended assembly each morning."

"Really, this used to be a school?"

"Yes, did the name not give it away?"

Jimmy shook his head looking confused.

Shadow sighed in despair and continued, "It was the York Ladies' College, an establishment dedicated to the education of our city's finest young females."

Jimmy looked around him, taking in the Victorian tiled floor, the high ceilings and the wood-panelled walls covered in many black-and-white photographs of sports teams and musical ensembles.

"It looks nothing like my old school."

Just then Francesco reappeared with the drinks and Shadow's prawns.

"Ah, Francesco, I was explaining to Sergeant Chang here, that this used to be a school."

"Yes, that's right. My father bought the place, maybe twenty-five years ago. It was still full of all the old junk when we took over. Some of it we kept—" he gestured towards the trophies on the mantelpiece and lacrosse sticks hanging from the ceiling "—but it took us weeks to clear the rest. When we were finally ready to open, my father asked Susie Slater, the famous singer, to cut the ribbon. She had been a pupil."

"I don't suppose you have any old photos of her from when she was here?" asked Shadow, his mouth already half full of prawns.

"Yes, certainly we do—they are in the ladies' cloakroom. I remember Susie made a joke of it at the time. She was a nice lady. I could send Lucia in to get them for you?" offered Francesco, as he turned to leave.

"No that's fine, Sergeant Chang can go," insisted Shadow.

Jimmy looked horrified. "Chief! What if someone's in there?"

"It'll be fine. Just show them your warrant card."

Reluctantly, Jimmy got up and self-consciously walked towards the ladies' toilets, leaving his boss to enjoy his starter.

SHADOW HAD JUST swallowed the last prawn, when Jimmy returned still looking sheepish and carrying several framed photographs under his arm. He slipped back into his chair and gave a relieved sigh.

"I found three with Susie in. You know she was really easy to spot. She hasn't changed that much."

Francesco hurried to clear the table, so the photographs could be laid out. The first showed the first eleven hockey team. Emma was sat in the middle as captain and Susie was standing on the back row. Shadow tapped his finger on the picture.

"That's Emma," he told Jimmy.

"Wow, she really was stunning. What a waste."

Shadow pushed his glasses on his nose and peered more closely at the photos. The second one was a class photo, showing twenty girls lined up in three rows, with a stern-looking, grey-haired woman in the middle of the front row and another younger woman next to her. The names of everyone were neatly printed below. Susie and Emma were standing next to each other in the middle row. The stern, older woman was Miss Robertshaw and the younger one Miss Brooke. The third photo was a less-staged image. Susie and Emma were being presented with a trophy for, according to the caption, winning the Yorkshire Ladies' Rowing Championship, but it wasn't the silverware Shadow was interested in, but the clearer image of a smiling and clapping Miss Brooke.

"It's her!" he exclaimed.

"Who?" asked Jimmy.

"Mad Alice!"

"Are you sure, sir?" Jimmy leaned forward and studied the two photographs more carefully.

"Definitely. Imagine her with grey hair and a bit thinner."

It was true. The delicate birdlike features and the shy, slightly nervous smile were unmistakable. Both men automatically looked out of the window, across the street to the narrow entrance of Mad Alice Lane, but she was nowhere to be seen. In fact, the whole street was unusually quiet. The sky had grown very dark and there was an ominous rumble of thunder in the distance. At the same time, the first few heavy drops of rain began to streak down the window.

"Maybe she used to be an English teacher and that's why she's always reciting poetry. Do you want me to go out and try to find her, sir?" Jimmy offered, but Shadow shook his head.

"No, leave her be. She's probably asleep by now anyway. We can talk to her in the morning. Hopefully, she'll be making more sense by then too."

Their view was suddenly blocked by a ghost tour, huddled under umbrellas, stopping outside their window. At the same time, Francesco arrived with the sea bass.

"Do any of the old teachers ever come in, Francesco?" enquired Shadow.

"No, sometimes students, old girls they call themselves, but not any teachers. Most must be very old or dead now. There is still Miss Hall, of course."

"Who's that?" asked Jimmy, as Shadow was already too absorbed with eating to continue the conversation.

"The old headmistress," explained Francesco, "she must

be nearly ninety now. She lived in one of the apartments upstairs and used to visit us from time to time. She liked to eat in the small dining room at the back; it had been her office. A few years ago, she moved out to Bishopthorpe, to a retirement home." He shook his head, sadly. "The poor lady had no family. I haven't seen her since she moved. Who knows, maybe she passed away."

Francesco made the sign of the cross before hurrying back into the kitchen. Shadow continued tucking into his fish enthusiastically, while Jimmy sipped his water thoughtfully.

"Why do you think Mad Alice, sorry I mean Miss Brooke, came back to York?" he asked.

Shadow shrugged.

"What do you think sent her loopy? Something that happened here?"

Shadow shrugged again.

Jimmy persisted. "Do you think Susie recognised her? She's pretty involved with most of the homeless in the city, but Miss Brooke wasn't at the soup kitchen tonight, was she?"

Shadow gave in. His sergeant clearly had no respect for a man when he was eating. Reluctantly, he lowered his knife and fork. "No, she wasn't, but earlier I saw her talking to Dr Stather down by the river. They looked fairly animated and I don't think it was the first time they had met."

Jimmy's eyes widened. "What do you think they were

talking about?"

"I've no idea. Now go and put those photos back where they belong and let me finish my dinner in peace."

BY THE TIME the two men left the restaurant, the heavens had definitely opened, and raindrops were pounding rapidly down on to the pavement. They wished each other good-night and Jimmy dashed around the corner, home to Goodramgate. Shadow turned up his collar and hurried back across the square and down Shambles, which was now eerily empty. He paused for a second outside the Angelique Boutique.

There was still a light on inside. When Shadow peered through the window, he could see Mandy and Cristina inside. Cristina was wearing a long red evening dress. She was standing with her hands on her hips and looking at her reflection in a mirror, while Mandy stood watching with folded arms, her expression impossible to read. Shadow was the first to admit he was no fashion expert, but he doubted Cristina was the boutique's usual type of customer. Both women turned their heads towards the corner of the room and Shadow guessed there was someone else present, but he couldn't see who. There was another rumble of thunder and a cold trickle of rain ran down his neck. He shivered and hurried on his way before either woman saw him.

CHAPTER FIVE

Across 10 (7 letters)
Getting the wrong idea in NYC can be deadly

THAT NIGHT SHADOW lay in his bed unable to sleep. He didn't know whether to blame his late-night snack of the half-eaten Stilton that had been lingering in the fridge, or his noisy neighbours. The geese who lived on the riverbank must have been excited by the earlier rain and were still honking loudly, long after the storm was over. He rearranged his pillows and closed his eyes again, but thoughts about the case kept jostling for prominence in his mind.

When he'd first moved back to York from London, he'd liked the way his home city had such a small-town feel, with everyone knowing everyone else. Right now, he found it claustrophobic. It was unsettling the way each person's life seemed to be entwined with the next person he met. The deaths of two young women, Fay and Emma, over thirty years apart, felt somehow connected. He couldn't see how, after all Emma must have been dead for years before Fay was even born, but it was just a feeling he had. A feeling that was keeping him awake. In the distance, he heard the bells of the

Minster chime five. It was pointless to try and sleep now; he may as well get up.

Half an hour later, he was showered, dressed and walking along the towpath. He passed the geese, who were now quiet and huddled together, sleeping peacefully. The old bonding warehouses, now converted into apartments, were all in darkness. The inky-black night sky was slowly turning a pale grey and a gentle mist was rising from the river. A cool breeze carried the scent of cocoa across the city, from the chocolate factory in the north. As he walked over Skeldergate Bridge, Shadow spotted two figures in sleeping bags huddled on the benches in the park below. He counted at least a dozen more similar figures in doorways as he wandered along Coppergate, Stonebow and Colliergate. The edges of the cardboard they slept on were dark and sodden from the heavy rain.

When he arrived back on Goodramgate, he paused at the spot where Fay had been found. Several bunches of flowers had been laid there in tribute. He knelt down and pulled out his glasses from his top pocket, so he could read the accompanying cards.

'Rest in Peace, Fay. You will always be in our hearts. With love from Luke, Susie and all your friends at The Haven.'

'Sleep with the Angels, sweet girl. Love from Cristina.'

'*Riposare in pace*—Gino and all at Catania's.'

Shadow straightened up with difficultly and removed his

glasses to rub his eyes. The sound of someone tapping on the glass behind him made him turn around. Gino was at the window of the restaurant and motioned for Shadow to come to the door. The two men knew each other well, as Catania's was another of Shadow's favourite Italian restaurants. They shook hands warmly and Gino handed the inspector an espresso.

"You are up early, my friend."

Shadow nodded as he sipped the coffee gratefully.

"I had a lot on my mind. How about you?"

"I'm waiting for a delivery of fish," Gino explained. "We closed yesterday out of respect for the unfortunate young girl, but today we must open. You understand?" He looked apologetic. Shadow smiled at him reassuringly.

"Of course. It was a kind gesture of you not to open."

"I wish there was something more we could have done. Maria and I weren't working that night—maybe if we had seen her, we could have helped. Maria has taken it badly. She is at mass right now."

Maria was Gino's wife. She was a small, fiery Sicilian and very religious.

"Who was working on Sunday night?"

"It was quiet by the end of the evening, so at closing time it was only Pepe—our manager—a chef and a young waitress. Your sergeant spoke to them all. They left after eleven, by the kitchen door at the back and went through Bedern, not Goodramgate. They said they didn't see anything."

Shadow drank down his coffee and waved Gino good-bye. The sun was up now, casting a warm golden glow on the pale cream stone of the Minster. He continued on his way past the great cathedral, deep in thought, and came to a stop outside St Wilfrid's, one of the city's few Catholic churches. Standing in the shadow of the Minster, it was dwarfed by its Anglican neighbour. He pushed open the heavy wooden door and stepped inside. There was a strong smell of incense and furniture polish. Down by the altar, a priest was conducting a quiet mass for a congregation of seven. Shadow could make out the figure of Gino's wife, Maria, her dark head bent in prayer.

Although not a religious man, at various times in his life Shadow had found the traditions of the church reassuring. Quietly, he made his way to a metal stand in the corner. Silently, he lit three candles, stood for a moment, then left as quickly as he'd arrived.

As he stepped outside and began walking towards Petergate, it occurred to him that Fay had probably been shown more kindness and respect in death, than she had in life. Both Fay and Emma had been called 'friend' by Susie Slater and both had died as teenagers. Was Jake right? Could Susie have been the target? Did somebody blame her for Emma's death?

Before he knew it, he found himself next to the entrance to Mad Alice Lane. Was it too early to wake her? Would she even understand his questions, or be able to answer them?

The last thing he wanted to do was upset her. He ducked his head under the entrance and took a few steps towards the body curled up on the velvet cushion. He gave a small cough and whispered, "Good morning." There was no response. He spoke again, a little louder, not wanting to startle her. "Good morning, Miss Brooke." He took another step towards her and reached out to touch her small, pale hand. To his horror, it was cold and lifeless. As he looked closer lying next to the body was a bottle of Holy Cow vodka.

CLUTCHING A LARGE takeaway coffee, Jimmy pushed his way through uniformed officers and forensics teams, while trying to dodge the crowd of complaining delivery drivers and business owners, who were being barred from getting on with their work. Shadow watched him approach as he sat alone on the steps of La Scuola Femminile, quietly sipping a cappuccino Francesco had brought out for him. He was silently berating himself. Instead of wasting time trying to find a connection between Fay and Emma, he should have been focused on who wanted to poison these poor souls sleeping on the streets. He drained his cup as his sergeant reached him.

"Sir, another body's been found," Jimmy said, urgently.

Shadow slowly raised his head. "For crying out loud, Jimmy, I know! It was me who found her."

"No, sir, not Mad Alice, I mean Miss Brooke. It's Norman."

Shadow paused for a second and then set his cup down and hauled himself up. "Where is he?"

"He was found in the alley next to The Snickel Side Inn. The landlord found him when he opened up this morning."

"Any chance it's natural causes?"

"I doubt it, sir. He was found with a half-empty bottle of Holy Cow."

"For crying out loud," muttered Shadow again, as he pushed his way back through the crowd with Jimmy close behind.

"Any comment, Mr Shadow?" shouted the familiar Scottish accent of Kevin MacNab. "Are these deaths connected to Fay Lawton?"

Shadow ignored the journalist and continued on, stony-faced.

A FEW STEPS past the Minster, where Low Petergate became High Petergate, stood The Snickel Side Inn. The landlord was waiting for them inside. His face was pale, and his hands were shaking as he gripped the large brandy in front of him. He explained that Norman often slept in the snickelway next to the pub that linked Petergate to Precentor's Court, particularly on wet nights.

Last night, he'd arrived quite early. The landlord could remember him turning up, but couldn't be sure of the time; however, it was definitely prior to eight o'clock because that's when the quiz started. At closing time, Norman usually tried to cadge a cigarette or some cash off the last of the customers to leave, but not last night. The landlord had assumed he'd sheltered from the thunderstorm and fallen asleep. When he came to open up this morning, he shouted to Norman to ask if he wanted a cup of tea, as he often did, and when he didn't reply the landlord went to investigate. That was when he discovered his body.

Shadow thanked the landlord and stepped outside with Jimmy. Then he went to take a look at the body before it was taken away. Like the other two victims, it was hidden in a dark, narrow snickelway off one of the city's busiest streets. Unlike Fay and Ruth Brooke, however, Norman looked quite peaceful and he was still clutching his almost-empty bottle of vodka tightly to his chest. Two members of the forensics teams were working round him.

"Fingerprints?" asked Shadow, without much hope.

"Only his," was the reply.

"What do you think, sir?" asked his sergeant.

Shadow sighed. "I think we can forget the idea that Fay's death was a mistake."

THE OUSE CRUISE Company were based next to Lendal Bridge. They offered a selection of self-drive small motorboats and rowing boats for tourists to hire, as well as running two large cruisers that went up and down the Ouse. One cruiser, the *Guy Fawkes*, chugged steadily away in the direction of Bishopthorpe. Sitting on the top deck, behind a party of noisy, excited schoolchildren were Shadow and Jimmy.

They were eating ice creams that Shadow had insisted on buying to cheer Jimmy up. He had a feeling his sergeant was sulking. Jimmy had wanted to question Eric Morrison, following the comments he'd made the previous evening about getting rid of all the city's homeless people. Jimmy also thought, as a brother with a younger sister, that Oliver should be informed that Emma had been found without any further delay. However, Shadow had insisted they needed to wait for confirmation from the dental records. He also didn't want to postpone the hastily arranged meeting they were now on their way to.

"I still don't know why you wouldn't let me drive us there, Chief," grumbled Jimmy, who didn't appear to be enjoying his ice cream very much.

"On a race day? The traffic will be terrible! This way we'll be there in ten minutes," replied Shadow confidently. He didn't mention his hatred of driving or being driven. "Maybe we should have brought those pictures you found last night, they might have helped to jog the old girl's memory."

"It's okay, sir, I photographed them with my mobile before I put them back." He held up the screen on his phone.

Shadow squinted at it and shook his head. "Really, Sergeant, she's ninety. She'll never be able to see that."

St Monica's Nursing Home had once been part of the Archbishop of York's sprawling estate and stood in the shadow of his palace. The well-manicured lawns stretched down to the river. The *Guy Fawkes* moored there briefly, letting any passengers who wanted to visit the palace off, before turning and heading back into the city.

Jimmy had phoned ahead, and Miss Geraldine Hall was waiting for them on the patio, sitting in a rattan chair under a large parasol. She was dressed in a pink and white striped linen dress, her grey hair was tightly curled, and she raised her large sunglasses on to her head as the two men approached. Shadow made the introductions and thanked her for seeing them.

"Not at all, Chief Inspector, thanks to you I shall be the envy of all the other residents. A visit from two members of the CID certainly trumps any of their grandchildren or even great-grandchildren. Now, do take a seat, gentlemen."

Shadow and Jimmy sat on the long, wooden bench that had been placed opposite her. She watched them with piercing blue eyes, making Shadow feel like they were a couple of naughty schoolboys. He shifted a little uncomfortably. It was another unusually hot day and the sun was dazzling him. It occurred to Shadow that anyone who didn't know better would think Miss Hall was the one conducting the investigation.

"We wanted to ask you about some events that happened approximately thirty-two years ago, when you were headmistress at York Ladies' College."

Miss Hall smiled and nodded encouragingly, as Shadow continued.

"Do you remember a young teacher named Ruth Brooke?"

"I have a picture on my phone if that would help?" offered Jimmy.

"Oh no thank you, Sergeant, that won't be necessary. I may sometimes struggle to recall where I left my reading glasses, but I remember all my girls and colleagues perfectly. Every single one of them. Miss Brooke came to us as a res grad as we used to say, a resident graduate. We took in two or three each year. New graduates, who were considering a career in teaching, would stay with us for a year and get a feel for the profession. They lived in and would assist the teaching staff and help run activities for the boarders at weekends or evenings. Sometimes they would supervise prep, that sort of thing. Ruth, I believe, was originally from Kent, but she gained a first at York, in English, and decided to stay on in the city. She was quiet, but well-liked by the staff and popular among the girls. Unfortunately, she suffered a sort of breakdown at the end of the summer term and left under a rather dark cloud."

"Was that the same summer term that Emma Harrison disappeared?" asked Shadow, gently.

The old lady's smile faded, and she appeared lost in her thoughts for a moment. Jimmy and Shadow glanced at each other, but then she spoke again with a sigh.

"Ah the wonderful Emma, such a waste. Nothing was ever quite the same after we lost her. As a teacher, I always tried very hard not to have favourites, but Emma was simply outstanding. An excellent scholar, musician, athlete and such a lovely sunny nature."

"Emma was the star pupil, not Susie?" asked Jimmy, in surprise.

Shadow frowned at him. He hated witnesses to be interrupted when they were in mid flow.

"Susie Slater? Emma's friend? Well she was gifted too, of course, and did very well in that singing competition on the television. I suppose many would call her a star. However, what you must remember, Sergeant, is the stars are always above us in the sky, but we don't see them when we are dazzled by the sun. Emma was the sun. It's as simple as that."

"Was Ruth Brooke involved in the disappearance of Emma?" asked Jimmy. Shadow thought he might have to strangle him.

"I suppose you could say that. I know she blamed herself and I believe that may have led to her breakdown. Emma and Susie were out training on the river. They had a county rowing competition coming up, I seem to recall. Located as we were in the city centre, the college didn't have its own boat shed of course, so we used St John's—no doubt it was seen as a chance by our girls for a little flirtation with their boys." She chuckled and Shadow and Jimmy smiled politely. "Emma and Susie were both very sensible and trustworthy, but still they needed supervision, and that is what Ruth was meant to be doing. Now to this day, I don't know exactly what happened. I suspect a young man may have been involved, but for whatever reason, when Emma fell in the river, Ruth was not there. She never gave a proper explanation of where she was, and she left us shortly afterwards.

"A few weeks later, I heard she had been admitted to some sort of institution back in Kent. Unfortunately, the college never really recovered from Emma's disappearance. Nor did it help that at the same time, some of the boys' schools in the city started to admit girls. You see, Chief Inspector, fathers will quite happily send their daughters to their son's school, but not the other way around. Within three years of Emma disappearing, we closed our doors for the last time." She leaned back in her chair with a heavy sigh. All of a sudden, she looked very tired.

Shadow stood up and thanked the headmistress for her

help, as Jimmy typed as quickly as he could in his notebook. They walked back to wait for the next city cruiser in silence. Shadow was mulling over what the old lady had told them. His thoughts were disturbed when Jimmy's phone suddenly bleeped. Jimmy retrieved it from his pocket and checked the screen.

"Only a text to confirm Kayleigh and Ryan were in custody all night. Kayleigh will have to serve the rest of her sentence, for breaking the terms of her release, but Ryan was released half an hour ago. I thought you'd want to rule them out, Chief."

Shadow nodded and was considering praising his sergeant for showing initiative, when there was another annoying bleep.

"What now?" he asked in irritation.

"It's a text from Sophie. She's checked the dental records and the body in Museum Gardens is definitely Emma."

"Has Sophie got Norman and Ruth too?" asked Shadow.

Jimmy tapped at his phone and a few seconds later, it bleeped in response. "She's got Norman; Donaldson has got Ruth."

"Oh well, you win some, you lose some," sighed Shadow.

WHEN THEY RETURNED to the city, Shadow finally allowed Jimmy to go and bring Eric Morrison in for questioning.

Meanwhile, now he had confirmation the body was definitely Emma, he could put off his visit to Oliver Harrison no longer. Her parents were both dead, so Oliver was the next of kin. As Shadow entered the wine shop, he found it was full of Dutch tourists enthusiastically enjoying the free samples, but a helpful young man directed him up a narrow staircase to where Oliver was in his office. When Shadow found him, he was sitting at his desk staring intently at his computer screen. Shadow knocked quietly on the already open door. Oliver stood up as soon as he saw him and stretched out his hand.

"Ah, Chief Inspector, come in, come in. Do have a seat. I've just been reading on the local news website that two more homeless people were found dead this morning. It's terrible, simply terrible!"

Shadow entered the office and sat in the comfortable leather chair in front of the desk, annoyed to hear the press was already reporting, no doubt inaccurately. "Unfortunately, yes and with more bottles of the same brand of vodka you sell here."

Oliver quickly held up his hands in protest. "I can promise you, Inspector, we haven't sold any since your last visit. In fact, I even asked Anthony to take the bottles we still had off the shelves, just to be safe. I've learned my lesson when it comes to that kind of thing."

"Please, Mr Harrison, that's not why I'm here." Shadow paused and took a breath. No matter how many times he did this, it never got any easier. "I came because we have found the body of your sister."

Oliver stared at him blankly for a second. Then he began blinking very quickly.

"Emma? Where?"

"In Museum Gardens, under the old boathouse."

To Shadow's horror, the bottom lip of the man opposite him began to quiver and tears started spilling down his face. Embarrassed, Shadow rummaged through his coat pockets before fishing out a slightly grubby white handkerchief, as Oliver's sobs echoed round the room. At the same time, Oliver produced a silk Paisley handkerchief from his top jacket pocket and began to dab his eyes furiously. Shadow glanced around the room while he waited for Oliver to compose himself.

On the walls were several small watercolours of vineyards and a large, low wooden bookcase was crammed with leather-bound wine reference books. In one corner was a pile of magazines called *Corkscrew*, next to another pile of the charity newspapers Byron sold. On the desk, next to some sheets of cream writing paper, were three framed photos. One of what Shadow assumed was Oliver as a little boy with his smiling parents and sister on a beach. Another showed his parents again, older and no longer smiling. The third was a black-and-white signed publicity shot of Susie from her days as a pop star.

"Forgive me, Chief Inspector." Oliver took several deep

breaths as he tried to calm himself. "This is quite a shock. I simply can't comprehend. She fell in the river. How could she have been under the boathouse all these years?"

"I understand, Mr Harrison. Investigations are still ongoing, but am I correct in saying that nobody actually saw Emma fall in the river?"

"Yes, that's right. Susie heard a splash, Emma was nowhere to be seen and well, obviously Susie put two and two together and panicked. She was in the water herself by the time I got there."

"You were there?" Shadow asked in surprise. There had been no mention of Oliver being present in the notes he'd read.

"Yes, I'd taken a year out before going to uni. My girlfriend at the time was working as an au pair in Amsterdam. I went to visit her for a while until I ran out of cash. Then I came home and got a summer job. The plan was to go back and travel round Europe, but well, with what happened..." He paused and blew his nose again before continuing. "I was selling ice creams from one of the carts by the entrance gates of Museum Gardens. I was just setting up and I knew the girls were down on the river, so when I heard Susie screaming, I dashed over as quickly as I could. When I arrived, Susie had already jumped in. I had to grab on to her oar and pull her out. Bless her, she wanted to keep looking for Em, but I could see she was struggling in the current. I'm sorry if I sound dim, Inspector, this is a lot to take in, but are you saying Em was killed? Her death wasn't an accident?"

"That's what we are investigating? Do you know why Emma didn't go into the boathouse to get changed at the same time as Susie?"

Oliver dabbed at his eyes and shook his head. "I think Em planned to meet up with Luke after training and I suppose Susie didn't want to play gooseberry, so she went in and changed alone."

"So, Luke was there as well?" Shadow was puzzled. There had been no witness statement on file from Luke either.

"Yes, but not until about ten minutes after me. We were frantic by then. He was too of course, when we told him what had happened."

"Luke and Emma were in a relationship at the time?"

Oliver's face broke into a smile. "Oh, they were mad about each other. Love's young dream! Had been for years. I used to tease Em about it. They even planned to go to the same uni. She wanted to study history and I think he was going to read English. Susie and I were the scientists, but as it turned out none of us made it to university. After Em disappeared, Mum and Dad needed me to help out here and Luke went completely off the rails. He started getting into drugs; he just totally lost it."

"And Susie went on to become rich and famous."

"Yes, that was weird. I can remember Susie talking about auditioning for the show with Emma. Not that Em would have done it—it wasn't her thing at all—but Susie really went for it and won. You know, Inspector, even with all the success and fame, Susie never gave up on Luke. She always came home to see how he was doing. She used to say she owed it to Emma to look after him."

"And the two of them got together?"

"Yes, well with Luke's dad being her manager, they saw a lot of each other. To be honest, I think Luke was pretty dazzled by the new glamorous Susie and her exciting new lifestyle. I have to admit I was a bit jealous. I'd always had a soft spot for Susie, used to hope the two of us, well you know…" He paused to wipe his eyes again and took a deep breath. "Look, Inspector, do you know when I'll be able to arrange a burial? I promised my mother, before she died, that if we ever found Emma, I'd have her buried in the same plot as her and Dad."

"I'll let you know as soon as I can, Mr Harrison." Shadow stood and shook Oliver's hand. As he turned to go, he stopped. "By the way, do you remember Ruth Brooke being down by the river the day Emma disappeared?"

Oliver frowned and thought for a moment. "Do you mean the teacher? Yes, she turned up a few minutes after me, looking very flustered. I don't recall her being much use— she just seemed to get into a flap. Why do you ask?"

"She was one of the bodies we found this morning."

Oliver raised his handkerchief to his mouth and shook his head sadly. "How strange. What on earth was she doing sleeping on the streets of York?"

"That's something else we need to investigate," Shadow replied.

SHADOW'S NEXT STOP on the Shambles was Mandy Morrison's Angelique Boutique. He took a deep breath before he pushed open the door. It wasn't a visit he was looking forward to. As he stepped inside, he was almost overwhelmed by a strong smell of perfume and dazzled by the glass chandeliers reflecting light on to the many mirrors around the room. The boutique was about as far from the shop's origins, as a medieval butcher's as it was possible to get. Rows of outfits and dresses, all covered in clear plastic, ran along the walls and a large glass table was in the centre. It was covered with carefully arranged handbags, jewellery and white roses in glass bottles.

Two assistants, who looked like mini Mandys with their stiff hair and heavy make-up, turned with expectant smiles when they saw him. The smiles faded when he loudly announced, "Chief Inspector Shadow to see Mrs Morrison."

One of the mini Mandys disappeared behind a red velvet curtain in the corner. The next thing Shadow heard was Mandy, in a loud and more refined voice than usual, saying, "Do excuse me a moment, Mrs Sherwin, while I leave you in Cheryl's capable hands." She appeared through the curtain scowling, sent the other mini Mandy scurrying away and marched over to Shadow.

"Well you've got a cheek coming here when I'm working, after that Chinese lad of yours carted poor Eric away," she hissed.

"Sergeant Chang and I are investigating three unexplained deaths, Mrs Morrison."

"And whose fault is that? Yours, Chief Inspector Shadow. If you had locked those vagrants up like we asked you to, they'd be safe and sound in a police cell, not dead on the street. Now you're trying to blame my Eric."

"Your husband was heard saying the homeless were vermin that should be exterminated."

"I thought we had freedom of speech in this country."

Shadow paused and held his tongue. He could see this conversation turning into an argument he would no doubt lose. Instead he changed tack. "I also wanted to ask you about the vodka you bought from Oliver Harrison earlier this year."

"What? Not that again. The fashion show was ages ago." Mandy's expression showed that she thought the policeman was quite mad.

"But you did buy some Holy Cow vodka?"

"Yes, one hundred little bottles for a fashion show. What's it got to do with you?"

"Did you hand them all out at the fashion show?"

"No, we gave away about thirty."

Shadow was a little surprised. Had she overestimated

how many people would attend the fashion show?

"So, what did you do with the other seventy?"

Mandy folded her arms defensively. "I tried to sell them back to Oliver, but the cheeky sod wouldn't take them. I don't know who he thinks he is. He's only got that business because he took it over from his poor father and mother."

It was the first time Shadow had heard her express any sympathy for another human being.

"Did you know his parents well?" he enquired.

Mandy's brittle features softened a little. "Anne Harrison was my first ever customer. She came in on the morning I opened and bought a silk scarf. I remember she wished me luck and said she liked to support local businesses. She was a nice woman, not a big spender, but she called in every few months. Then she lost her girl and was never the same again. Neither of them were. Emma was a lovely girl, absolutely stunning. She was the light of their lives. When she disappeared, well they may as well have died too."

"But they still had Oliver."

"Huh, that useless lump?" Mandy's expression hardened again. "Oliver has always been a wimp. He couldn't hold a candle to Emma. Everyone knew she was the favourite."

"So, what happened to the leftover vodka?" Shadow persisted, as Mandy rolled her eyes.

"We drank it."

"All of it? Can you prove that?"

"No, of course I can't. Gin's my normal tipple, but that

stuff cost me a small fortune. If you stick it in a Diet Coke, it tastes all right."

"Just so you know, I'll be asking for a search warrant for here and your home address, so don't go anywhere will you, Mrs Morrison."

"Go anywhere? How dare you? I've been here for over thirty years, paying my rent and rates. Paying your wages— and this is how I'm treated."

Shadow turned to leave. He had no intention of requesting a search warrant, but he was interested in Mandy's reaction. She was still ranting at him, as he walked out the door.

As ALWAYS, HIS progress back down the Shambles was slow. He had often thought the city should consider introducing a traffic system for pedestrians. A slow lane for tourists who wanted to take their time—to stop, stare and photograph the city's treasures—and a fast lane for locals wanting to go about their business. The gnawing feeling in his stomach reminded him that it was almost lunchtime, and that he'd also missed out on his usual breakfast. Bettys would be far too busy now, and as much as he liked the place, he didn't feel like queuing. Instead he headed back down to the river, picking up a *Yorkshire Post* on the way. His mood wasn't improved when he saw in the newsagent's window, the

Herald's front page proclaiming, 'Serial Killer On The Streets.'

SHADOW ARRIVED AT The King's Head a few minutes before twelve, but the unusually sunny weather meant it was already busy. He managed to find an empty seat at a table on the cobbles by the river and ordered a ploughman's and a pint of Black Sheep. Unfolding his newspaper, he ignored the front page that was running the story about Fay and turned straight to the crossword.

Ten minutes and only five clues later, he was struggling to concentrate. There was something about his visit to the boutique that was bothering him, but he wasn't sure what. He removed his reading glasses and rubbed his tired eyes. If he looked down the river and squinted, he could almost see *Florence* beyond the bridge. Maybe he should have bought a sandwich and gone home for lunch. It was too noisy here to think.

A flash of white and pink on the other side of the river suddenly caught his eye. He squinted again. It was Cristina wearing a bright pink top and her platinum-blonde hair glinting in the bright sun. She was walking very quickly along the old path with two men. Shadow thought one of them might be Ryan. Jimmy said he'd been released, but he didn't recognise the other tall, well-built, bald man. His line of sight was suddenly blocked by the waitress arriving with his lunch and when he looked again, all three had disappeared.

He ate quickly. The laughing and chatting students and tourists seemed to be getting louder by the minute. To make matters worse, he begrudgingly had to share his table with some Australian backpackers. As soon as he'd finished, he went inside to pay the bill. On the bar, next to the till, were a selection of glass jars and bottles with handwritten labels. The barman saw Shadow studying them.

"That's the pickle you had with your ploughman's, if you want a jar. The landlord's wife makes it herself," he explained, hopefully.

"What's in the bottles?"

"Damson gin and sloe gin. Would you like a bottle?"

Shadow frowned and shook his head.

"Do you know where she gets them from? The bottles I mean, not the sloes and damsons."

"I'll go and ask in the kitchen," replied the barman, looking a little puzzled. He returned a few moments later.

"She said they're from Barnitts."

Shadow thanked him, paid the bill and left. He was sure those bottles were the same as the ones the murderer had put the vodka in and given to the victims, but Barnitts was the most popular homeware store in the city. Unless they kept exact records of who bought what and when, it wasn't going to be much help. Halfway up the steps from the pub to the bridge, he stopped suddenly. It was the bottles. The thing that had been bothering him since he left the boutique. The white roses on the circular table were in the same glass bottles.

With a sense of relief, he continued on his way, wondering if a visit to Barnitts would be worthwhile, or a waste of time. First though, he would need to find a chemist's shop. His lunch was already calling out for a new supply of indigestion tablets.

As he was about to cross the road he suddenly stopped. Coming out of the chemist's opposite was Luke Carrington, closely followed by Oliver Harrison holding a large carrier bag. Luke was talking animatedly on his mobile. Shadow wondered why he was holding the phone in his right hand, but as he turned slightly, he saw his left hand was wrapped in bandages. Oliver, who had been impeccably dressed when Shadow had last seen him, now looked dishevelled to say the least. His jacket was off, his shirt was untucked, and his sleeves were rolled up. Shadow strained his eyes. He was almost certain there were bloodstains on the front of Oliver's clothes.

He waited and watched the two men walk away. He decided Barnitts and the glass bottles would have to wait.

CHAPTER SIX

Down 2 (10 letters)
By going through the narrow passage, the lackey wins his prize

S USIE SLATER WAS perched on the reception desk, wearing a pretty floral sundress when Shadow arrived. She was waiting for him with a bright smile and a cup of freshly brewed coffee.

"Hello, Chief Inspector, goodness what a day you must be having. I thought you might be in need of caffeine?"

She patted him affectionately on the shoulder, as she handed the coffee over.

"You knew I was coming?" asked Shadow in surprise, feeling himself blush slightly.

"Thanks to the all-seeing eye!" Susie pointed to the monitor behind the desk. It showed a grainy, black-and-white image from the front door.

"I don't suppose it records as well does it?" asked Shadow, thinking back to the night Fay left.

"I'm afraid not. It's a bit of an antique. I suppose with everything that's happened we should really get it upgraded."

"I take it you've heard about the two deaths that occurred last night?"

"Yes, it's so awful. I was only talking to poor old Norman at the soup kitchen last night. It's such a shame. I know most people thought he was a lost cause, but he was sweet in his own way." She sighed heavily. "Although, to be quite honest with you, Chief Inspector, as sorry as I am about what happened to Norman and the other lady, I'm more upset to hear you've finally found Emma."

"Who told you?" Shadow asked, although he was certain he already knew the answer.

"Oliver. He phoned us in such a state that we both dashed over to his office. He's still with Luke now. Those two are really struggling with the news. Even after all these years, I think they both still hoped there was a chance she might come back. Oliver, I know, has always felt guilty."

"Why should Oliver feel guilty?"

"He and Emma had always been close, but before Em disappeared he'd been quite unkind to her. Emma was really upset about it. I think it was just a bit of sibling rivalry. I'm an only child, so I wouldn't know, but Ollie's exam results weren't all he'd hoped for and their parents were so excited about Em applying to Oxford. It was all their dad could talk about and I...well I just think it got to Ollie."

Susie paused and took a breath, her eyes bright with tears. "I simply can't understand it. How did Emma get in the tunnel? Could the current have carried her there? When the river was high, during the floods perhaps?"

Shadow smiled politely but didn't say that they doubted Emma's body had ever entered the water. He was more interested in her reaction to recent events.

"I saw Luke earlier. He's hurt his hand."

Susie glanced away briefly. For once, she didn't seem to know what to say. When she turned back to Shadow her usually bright eyes looked tired and dull.

"Yes, did you speak to him?"

"No, he was on the other side of the road, leaving the pharmacy when I saw him," Shadow explained, and Susie smiled and seemed to relax again.

"Oh, his hand was just a silly accident. He cut it on a broken glass at Ollie's. He must have been collecting his tablets when you saw him. I expect he will need them more than ever after today's terrible news. Poor thing!"

"May I ask what tablets he takes?"

"Valium, to help keep him calm, and sleeping tablets. He takes one every night at 10pm on the dot. He'd never cope without them."

Shadow recalled Luke's comment about being dead to the world the night Fay was killed.

"Did Oliver also tell you that the homeless lady we found this morning was Ruth Brooke?"

"Who?"

"Ruth Brooke—you may remember her as Miss Brooke."

Susie wrinkled her forehead for a few seconds. "You mean Miss Brooke the res grad from school? Goodness!

What on earth was she doing in York? The last we heard she was down south in a hospital or somewhere? She had a breakdown, you know?"

"Yes, it seems she returned to the city a couple of months ago. You never recognised her or spoke to her? She often sat in Petergate, opposite your old school."

"No, I'm afraid not, Chief Inspector. I can vaguely recall seeing an older lady there; perhaps I should have approached her, but I never thought it was someone I might know. She never came here or to our soup kitchens."

"Oliver said Miss Brooke was in Museum Gardens on the day Emma disappeared."

Susie sighed and brushed her hair away from her eyes. "She was meant to be supervising us, but she wandered off while we were on the river. Neither of us minded her not being there. She was a bit of a dreamer and quite shy, Chief Inspector. The younger girls used to run rings around her. I'm afraid when she did reappear, she wasn't much use. She just panicked."

"I see." Shadow paused. "Oliver Harrison also mentioned you bought some Holy Cow vodka for Mr Carrington's birthday party."

Susie rolled her eyes dramatically and groaned. "Oh, what a disaster that was! Luke completely freaked out because it wasn't vegan!"

"So, what happened to the vodka?" asked Shadow.

Susie gave him a conspiratorial grin and whispered, "I've

hidden it from Luke in the office. I'm going to wait until September then make bramble vodka and give it as Christmas presents. I've already got the bottles and ribbons ready. Hopefully Luke will have forgotten all about it by then. If not, I shall have to try and persuade him it would be a waste not to use it."

"Would it be possible to see the vodka?"

Susie looked a little taken aback. "Of course. It's down in my office, in the basement. Can you hold the fort here, Jess?" she called to the girl with bright pink hair, who had been quietly rearranging the leaflets on the noticeboard. Shadow followed Susie through a door and down some steep stone steps into the basement office.

"How did you feel about the petition Mrs Morrison organised, against the soup kitchen? I assume you knew about it?" he asked. Susie glanced over her shoulder.

"Water off a duck's back to me, Chief Inspector. The world is full of NIMBYs. You should have seen the objections the council received when we wanted to open this place." She put her hand on the door handle, paused and turned to Shadow. "But now I come to think of it, I mean in the light of what's happened, perhaps we should have taken the petition more seriously. After all, someone is obviously targeting the homeless. Mr and Mrs Morrison were both very angry last night. Have you spoken to them?"

"Don't worry, Miss Slater, we are looking at the petition and those who signed it."

"Of course, you are, Chief Inspector, and I told you, please call me Susie."

She pushed open the door. The office was a messy, chaotic room with piles of papers and potted plants covering two desks. The fluorescent light flickered unreliably and there was a slight draught coming from the partly open window, overlooking the yard. Susie followed Shadow's gaze.

"Luke's been promising to fix it for ages, but DIY isn't really his thing," she explained, as she rattled a key in the lock of a tall, thin, metal cupboard. She opened it with difficulty and then knelt down and began rummaging on the bottom shelf.

"Ah here it is, Chief Inspector," she said, triumphantly, as she pulled out a white box still sealed with the Bacchus-branded tape.

"Let me open it for you," she offered, grabbing a pair of large scissors from the desk. She sliced through the tape and opened the box, showing Shadow the neatly packed miniature bottles inside. "All present and correct." She picked out two bottles and handed one to Shadow. She opened hers and with a sad smile, said quietly, "Let's drink to absent friends!" She gently tapped her bottle against Shadow's, then took a long swig. Shadow opened his bottle a little more cautiously and took a sniff. It was definitely vodka, so returning her smile, he raised his bottle too.

"To absent friends!"

WHEN HE RETURNED to the station, Shadow found Jimmy sitting in front of his laptop. His long dark fringe had flopped over his eyes as he stared intently at the screen. He was tapping the image with the end of his pen as he counted out loud. Shadow stood behind him and cleared his throat loudly. Jimmy turned around looking startled.

"Sorry, Chief, I was concentrating on last night's CCTV footage," he apologised.

"So, I see," said Shadow. "What have you got?"

"Lots to report," replied Jimmy eagerly reaching for his digital notebook.

"Right, well bring that and that—" Shadow pointed to the laptop and notebook "—to my office. I'm going to get a cup of tea from the canteen." The vodka had left a nasty aftertaste in his mouth. He was almost out of the door before he thought to turn around.

"Do you want anything?" he asked.

Jimmy, who was a bit of a coffee aficionado, pulled a face and shook his head. "No thanks, Chief. Not from the canteen."

"Please yourself," muttered Shadow.

A few moments later, Shadow returned carrying a cup of tea that he had to admit did resemble dishwater. He found Jimmy, notebook and laptop in hand, waiting patiently outside his office.

"You could have gone in you know, Sergeant?" he said, pushing the door open and flicking on the lights. His office was even more sparsely furnished than *Florence*. Although he'd moved in over fifteen years ago when he was promoted to chief inspector, there were no photos, plants or even a calendar on the wall. The only personal effects in his desk drawers were a few old copies of *The Yorkshire Post*, with unfinished crosswords and a half-empty packet of indigestion tablets.

"Sorry, Chief. Like I said, quite a lot to report," said Jimmy enthusiastically, as he followed his boss inside.

Shadow flopped wearily into his chair and motioned for Jimmy to sit opposite him. "Well off you go then."

Jimmy opened up his laptop and entered the code on his notebook, ignoring Shadow's loud, deliberate sigh.

"Firstly, we had to let Morrison go. He had an alibi. He said after the soup kitchen was over, he went straight to Ted's bar and sank more than a few pints there."

"Could anyone back him up?"

"Oh yes, Ted was falling over himself to assure us Eric was there all night."

"I see." Shadow raised an eyebrow. In his experience, Ted rarely helped anyone unless there was something in it for him. "What's next?"

"I managed to trace the last hospital where Ruth Brooke was treated. She had no next of kin, by the way. Oh, and nor does Norman, but I think we probably knew that already.

The doctor at Ruth's hospital said she was discharged three months ago. She had been responding well to treatment and he had no idea she was planning on returning to York. From his records, he said in the past whenever this city or her time here was mentioned, Ruth became distressed or sometimes even had a relapse. However, according to her records, she never gave any further details about what happened on the day Emma disappeared."

"Anything else?"

"The chief constable has been on. She said she's due to make a statement to the press. Three unexplained deaths in York is a big deal, so she wants an update from you."

Shadow frowned. He tried to avoid the chief constable at all costs. Fortunately, she was based out at the county headquarters in Northallerton, so their paths didn't often cross.

"Any good news?"

"Sort of. I've managed to access the CCTV that covers Petergate for last night—that's what I was looking at be-fore—and Sophie has narrowed down the time of death to between eight and nine last night."

"That's about the time we left the restaurant, when the storm started. Did you see anything on the CCTV?"

"I think so. Let me show you." He tapped on the lap-top's keyboard while Shadow took a sip of tea, then put his glasses on. They both squinted at the slightly blurred images on the screen. Shadow saw they were looking at Petergate early yesterday evening. It was thronged with tourists and shoppers. He also spotted a few from the soup kitchen too, volunteers as well as those wanting to be fed.

"Now, if I fast-forward to when the storm starts…" said Jimmy, as his long thin fingers rapidly tapped the keyboard. The image grew much darker and the street was almost empty. Shadow glanced at the clock in the corner of the screen. They were now at the time the murders were meant to have taken place. The odd figure hurried by, but their features were all obscured by umbrellas or hoods. It was impossible to even tell if they were male or female. However, none of them stopped by the entrance to Lund Court.

"Keep watching, Chief, here comes the ghost tour."

"The one we saw from the restaurant window?" Shadow asked and Jimmy nodded as he turned his attention back to his notebook.

"Yes, I contacted the man who runs the tour to confirm the route and check the numbers. He's called Steve and seemed like a nice guy. He told me nobody booked in advance, they just turned up at the advertised spot at the top of Shambles and paid their five pounds. Last night, there had been sixteen for the tour, a mixture of Americans, Australians, English and possibly a Dutch couple, although he couldn't be sure because of the accent—they might have been German."

Shadow groaned loudly and Jimmy hurried on.

"The tour usually lasts an hour and a half. He stopped a

total of six times to tell ghost stories along the way, including the one about Mad Alice. Due to the terrible weather, not all of them made it to the end, with quite a few disappearing into pubs along the way. He also said it was possible others had tagged along without him noticing—apparently that happens quite often. He said, and I quote, 'They're either foreigners, who don't know what's going on, or cheeky buggers, who want a tour without paying.'"

"All right, all right, I don't need to know the inner workings of the ghost tour business, Sergeant," sighed Shadow, holding his hand up in protest.

Jimmy retrieved a pen he'd tucked behind his ear and tapped on the screen. "So, I've been trying to count feet. With so many of the crowd using umbrellas it was no good trying to count heads. I am fairly certain that when they left Kings Square, I counted seventeen pairs of feet, including the tour guide. Now when I click to the next image, taken a little bit further along from Francesco's restaurant, I am sure there's an extra person. I've counted four times now, Chief. Each time I get the same result."

The lines around Shadow's eyes deepened as he squinted at the screen. Jimmy was right about the pairs of feet. Was it possible the killer could have murdered Ruth, then brazenly stepped out of Lund Court after the guide told the story of the real Mad Alice?

Jimmy turned to him. His expression had clouded. "I've been thinking, Chief. If I'd gone to see Ruth after we found those photographs of her, she might still be alive."

Shadow patted him on the shoulder, a little awkwardly. A similar thought had crossed his mind. "And I stopped you, I know. You can't blame yourself for what happened, Sergeant. All we can do now is find out who killed her. So, let's crack on."

Jimmy flicked to the next image of the group as they passed by the Minster. "You see here, there's definitely still eighteen pairs of feet. According to Steve, they made their way down to Treasurer's House, then round the back of the Minster to rejoin Petergate and finish the tour around the corner, outside the Theatre Royal. The next image of the group I've got is when they are about to go through Bootham Bar. At this point, they would have passed by The Snickel Side Inn and the snickelway where Norman was sleeping. Now there are only fifteen pairs."

Jimmy tapped on the screen once more then dropped his pen on the desk and took a step back so Shadow could see more clearly for himself.

"Where have three of them disappeared to?" asked Shadow, frowning. He did a quick tally in his head. There was one restaurant and four pubs on that stretch of Petergate, including The Snickel Side Inn. Had they just ducked into one of those, or had one, or all three paid Norman a visit?

He turned to Jimmy. "You'd better check with the restaurants and bars along there. It's a long shot but see if anyone can remember something relevant."

"Will do," said Jimmy, folding away the laptop. "By the way, how did it go with Oliver Harrison, Chief?"

Shadow was about to reply, when the telephone on his desk rang. Shadow pointed to it.

"You answer it. If it's the chief constable, tell her I'm not here."

Jimmy sighed and picked up the receiver.

"Hello?" He paused for a moment before smiling and handing the receiver to Shadow. "It's Dr Donaldson for you, sir."

"Yes," barked Shadow, scowling at his sergeant.

"Ah, Shadow, I've managed to track you down. I'm off to the Algarve tomorrow, so I wanted to put this business to bed. I'll have Miss Habbershaw send the full report to you while I'm away. This vagrant is almost identical to the other one you sent me, but older of course. I put her age at around fifty. She was a little underweight, but no signs of previous drug use. Toxicology shows same type and amount of cyanide compound as before. The one mildly interesting detail, is that there was bruising around her nose and mouth and each of her fingernails were broken."

"Meaning?"

"Meaning she didn't drink the vodka voluntarily. In fact, looking at her liver I doubt she drank at all. She attempted to fight back, but her nose was held and her mouth forced open, and the liquid poured down." Donaldson chuckled. "It rather reminded me of when Nanny tried to make me take my castor oil."

Shadow didn't find this anecdote even slightly amusing, but thought it went a long way to explaining Donaldson's personality.

When Shadow put the receiver down, it rang again almost immediately. He picked it up without thinking. This time it was the chief constable. Jimmy diplomatically left the office, as her shrill voice echoed down the line.

She told Shadow in no uncertain terms that she expected results and quickly. The local MP and leader of the city council had been in contact with her. Both had reminded her that York relied heavily on the income from tourism. These three deaths not only highlighted the city's homeless problem but led the press to start throwing around unhelpful phrases like 'serial killer on the loose.' Shadow recalled the *Herald*'s front page. The chief constable insisted she expected a speedy resolution before businesses were affected.

Shadow resisted the temptation to say that had the leader and MP worked harder to solve the problem of homelessness, they might not be faced with the problem of these deaths now. Instead, he suggested that when the chief constable spoke to the press she focused on the discovery of Emma's body after over thirty years. Those local residents with long memories might recall the case. She reluctantly agreed and made him promise not to speak to the press himself.

"Tact is not your strong point, Shadow," she stated firmly, ending the conversation.

Shadow was more than happy to comply with her request. Over the years, he had turned down all offers to go on media training courses, and he intended to keep it that way, especially if it meant he could avoid talking to young Mr MacNab.

THE POLICE STATION was housed in the old Medieval Guildhall, in the heart of the city and on the edge of the river. After his conversation with the chief constable, Shadow decided he needed to see a friendly face, so he made his way up to the records office. It had originally been decided to locate it in the tower room, with the hope that even during the worst floods, being so high would help keep all the files and documents safe. Sergeant George Hedley was in charge of the station's records office and was also one of the city's longest-serving officers. He peered over his glasses in surprise when he saw Shadow breathlessly trudging towards his desk.

"To what do we owe this honour, John? It's not like you to grace us with your presence."

Shadow, still trying to catch his breath, flopped into the chair opposite his old friend.

"You know, George, you should really think of getting them to install a lift for up here. Those stairs will kill somebody one day."

"Speak for yourself." The sergeant laughed. "We're not all as knackered as you. Besides, you usually send one of your minions up here if you want something."

"Well, the last file you sent down was no good. Half of the information was missing."

"The Emma Harrison file was complete," George insisted, bristling slightly. He prided himself on maintaining perfectly all the records in his care.

"I've got two witnesses who didn't give witness statements, or if they did, they aren't in your file."

"Don't start blaming us. We can only file what we're given. What witnesses?"

"The victim's brother, Oliver, and her boyfriend, Luke Carrington."

"Minors?"

"The brother no, but it's possible Luke may still have been seventeen at the time."

Sergeant Hedley placed the tips of his fingers together in front of him as he thought for a moment. Shadow could almost see the cogs of his memory begin to turn.

"Luke Carrington? Son of Den Carrington? And Oliver Harrison. Both were pupils at St John's?" Shadow nodded and George gave a short snort of laughter. "Well I think that explains it. Your predecessor, DCI Grunwell, as I'm sure you've heard, was one of the funny handshake brigade. So were Den and Nigel Taylor-Dunn, headmaster of St. John's at the time."

Shadow groaned. This wasn't the first time he'd encountered a problem created by Grunwell and his dubious methods of investigation. He'd seemed more concerned with doing favours for friends than solving crimes.

"Any particular reason for them wanting to hush things up?"

George closed his eyes, deep in thought once again. "It was a long time ago, John, but a big case at the time. I seem to remember the Carrington boy was adamant he'd seen something that he thought could have been a body in the river, when he was on his way to meet Emma. He was supposed to be on a cross-country run around the city. Unfortunately, he'd been smoking some fairly heavy-duty weed with a classmate beforehand, so he was an unreliable witness to say the least."

"Did he say where he got the weed from?"

George shook his head. "I think we worked out it must have been another pupil or former pupil. Either way, it was hushed up. St John's was about to begin accepting girls and the last thing they wanted was any bad publicity."

Shadow recalled how Miss Hall had described the way York Ladies' College had suffered, and ultimately closed following Emma's disappearance.

"So Grunwell arranged for their statements to be lost?" Shadow sighed and stood up wearily. As he did, he noticed a photo on the desk of George and his wife holding a baby.

"Are you a grandad now, George?"

"It was six weeks ago. Lucy had a little boy," George said, his voice full of pride. "The christening is this Sunday. Carol wanted to ask you, but don't worry, I told her it wasn't your sort of thing."

Shadow leant over and shook his old friend's hand.

"Congratulations! You see, George, it was worth nearly killing myself to come up here. I don't know why they bother with all these boxes of files; we just need you and your memory."

"Flattery will get you everywhere. Now are you going to manage the stairs, or should I phone the air ambulance to get you down?"

CHAPTER SEVEN

Down 3 (6 letters)
Partly redefining a close ally

S HADOW AND JIMMY left the station together that evening. As they walked across St Helen's Square, Shadow updated his deputy regarding his conversations with Oliver, Mandy, Susie and George.

"So, Luke was into drugs even before Emma died? I can see why they wouldn't want him on record as a witness, but I don't understand why they got rid of Oliver's statement," queried a puzzled Jimmy.

"I have a feeling he might have been the one supplying Luke," explained Shadow. Jimmy raised an eyebrow in surprise. "Really, Chief? He doesn't seem the type."

"There was something he said today about learning his lesson, made me wonder. He also mentioned his girlfriend was in Amsterdam at the time Emma disappeared. Maybe he bought it there legally, then brought it back home. The statements he and Luke had given might have implicated each other, so they were removed."

"All these years Luke thought he saw a body in the river

and realised too late it might have been his girlfriend? Living with the guilt of not having done anything. It's no wonder he's a bit weird, Chief."

Shadow nodded. He thought about Luke and his bandaged hand and wondered how he had really reacted when he heard Emma had never been in the river at all.

SINCE JIMMY BEGAN working for him, Shadow had fallen into a routine of eating at his family's restaurant once a week. The Golden Dragon was part of 'Our Lady Row,' a stretch of Goodramgate containing some of the oldest houses in the city. The kitchen was on the ground floor and the main seating area of the restaurant was up a winding staircase, on the first floor. Traditional red Chinese lanterns were strung along the low, dark beams, carved with the date 1316 and large, ornately decorated fans filled the ancient fireplace. The floor above the restaurant was where the family lived.

Jimmy's mother, Rose, excited at her son's promotion and horrified to hear a chief inspector ate alone every evening, insisted on inviting him to dine with them. So now, much to Jimmy's embarrassment, every Wednesday evening, Shadow arrived to eat beef in black bean sauce with fried rice. He sat at the table next to the kitchen, on the ground floor. It was Jimmy's grandfather's table, but Shadow, who as Jimmy had tried to explain preferred to dine alone, was quite happy. The elderly gentleman spoke no English and Shadow didn't know any Chinese, so they ate in comfortable silence. Waitresses and diners bustled past them and the clatter of pans and chatter of the Chinese chefs in the kitchen kept them entertained.

Then, after dinner, the two men played a game of backgammon, and Shadow invariably lost. Sometimes Jimmy ate with them, but he was often called away by his mother, who spent the evening dashing between customers, her family and the kitchen.

This evening, however, they were also joined by Jimmy and his younger sister, Angela, who was training to become a teacher. Jimmy had set his laptop on the table so they could all watch the chief constable's news conference. Angela rapidly translated what was being said for her grandfather. As Shadow had suggested, the chief constable only briefly touched on the three most recent deaths. The victims' three pictures were shown, the one of Ruth showed her when she was at the college and the chief constable merely said investigations into the three deaths were ongoing and she asked the public to come forward if they had seen anything. She then moved swiftly on to appealing for information regarding the discovery of Emma, who had been presumed missing for thirty-two years.

"Who's going to remember what they were doing thirty-two years ago?" tutted Angela. Shadow smiled to himself. To someone Angela's age, thirty-two years probably sounded like a lifetime, to him it often felt like yesterday.

"Have you given up on the idea Emma's death is linked to Fay's, Chief?" asked Jimmy, as he cleared away the laptop.

Shadow sighed. "I think so. The only thing that linked them was being found on the same day, but now it seems like the homeless are definitely being targeted."

"I don't know," said Angela thoughtfully, "I still think it's odd Susie Slater was the last person to see both Emma and Fay alive."

Jimmy rolled his eyes at her. "I think you'll find, Sis," he explained condescendingly, "in each case it was their murderer who was the last person to see them alive."

"Whatever, Sherlock!" his sister replied sarcastically. Jimmy carried the laptop away. Angela pulled a face at him as he left, and she returned to designing what looked like a poster covered in small white owls. Her grandfather tapped on the poster and asked her something. Angela replied to him, then turned to Shadow politely.

"Granddad asked me what I was doing. I have just explained to him that I am running a lunchtime Chinese club, at the school where I'm doing my training. Tomorrow, the children are coming here to try some Chinese food and practise some phrases they have been learning. I'm going to print off some menus for them and put this puzzle on the back. You see amongst the owls, one cat is hidden. They actually have quite similar facial features. The children have to try and find the cat. It also works as a joke, a play on words. You see the word for cat in Chinese is '*mao*' a bit like the noise they make, and for owl is '*mao tou ying.*' It literally translates as 'cat head eagle.'"

"Now your turn, Chief Inspector," said Rose, Jimmy's mother, who had suddenly appeared at the kitchen door. She smiled at Shadow expectantly and Shadow knew she was waiting for him to attempt to pronounce the words. Angela and Rose never missed an opportunity to try and teach him a Chinese word or phrase, much to the amusement of Jimmy and his grandfather.

"*Mao tou ying,*" he muttered obediently, feeling very self-conscious. Angela and Rose beamed and applauded, as the grandfather chuckled and removed another of Shadow's checkers from the board.

"Very good, Chief Inspector," said Rose, before disappearing back into the kitchen. Shadow, feeling embarrassed, frowned. Despite the impromptu language lesson, something Angela had said was bothering him. A puzzle. One cat hidden amongst the owls.

"Maybe that's it," he said out loud.

"Chief?" asked Jimmy, who had just returned to the table and hadn't heard the conversation with his sister.

"What if only one of the homeless victims was the real target? They weren't all linked. The other two were just a distraction."

"Collateral damage you mean?" asked Jimmy.

"Well if you insist on using these American terms you've

picked up."

Angela who was again translating for her grandfather, stopped and laughed.

"You might work for NYPD, Jimmy, but you need to remember that it's North Yorkshire not New York Police Department." She turned to Shadow. "So who was the real target, Chief Inspector? Norman, Fay or Ruth?"

Shadow shrugged. "I wish I knew, Angela."

"Surely you don't think it can be Norman, Chief?" asked Jimmy. "I'm not sure he even knew what day it was most of the time. As for Ruth, she never made any sense either. I know it's strange her suddenly turning up in York again, then Emma being found, but it could just be coincidence."

"So, you think it's all about Fay?" asked Shadow.

"It's got to be, sir. She was supplying drugs. Ted knew her, Eric drank in the same place as her and they've both got previous. I'm sure there's more going on there than we know about."

"You might be right, Sergeant," said Shadow with a yawn. The lack of sleep was beginning to catch up with him.

Angela gave a shudder as she returned to drawing her owls. "Well I don't know which is worse, a serial killer who has a grudge against the homeless or a psycho who murders people as a distraction."

Neither did Shadow and he'd been so preoccupied he hadn't noticed Jimmy's grandfather had quietly finished bearing off. The two men shook hands over what had been

Shadow's speediest defeat to date. He thanked Rose, who as always made him promise to return next week, and he said goodnight to the others. He headed back to *Florence*, tired and hoping for an uninterrupted night's sleep.

AT BETTYS THE next morning, Shadow was enjoying his breakfast even more than usual, having missed it the previous day. He was so engrossed he didn't even see Jimmy sliding into the seat opposite him.

"Morning, sir, looks like you might have been right to stay focused on Emma, after all. There was a call overnight from Australia. A lady in Perth whose daughter is studying over here and saw the chief constable on TV and emailed her mum about it."

"And?" asked Shadow, not bothering to look up from his plate.

"It turns out the mother was another resident graduate at York Ladies' College, at the same time as Ruth Brooke. She says she remembers Ruth as clever and kind, but a bit shy and naïve, and quite young for her age. Apparently, she treated Susie and Emma in particular more as friends than pupils. She also said Ruth was seeing a man and that she was 'head over heels in love' with him. The lady from Australia didn't know his name, but—" Jimmy paused as if for dramatic effect "—he was an archaeologist."

Shadow looked up, his fork halfway to his mouth. "Stather!"

"*Doctor* Stather, Chief!" Jimmy replied with a grin.

THE YORK HISTORIC Foundation's offices were accessed through a small door in the Shambles between Mandy's boutique and a shop selling handmade fudge. Shadow kept his head down as he passed the former, not wishing to have another altercation with either of the Morrisons right now. He pressed the button for the intercom. A crackly voice told him to come up and the door buzzed, then clicked open.

He made his way up a narrow staircase, to a landing where a small grey-haired lady dressed all in black was waiting for him. She led him through a tiny office with a low ceiling and uneven floor, to a large wooden door with a gleaming brass plaque bearing Stather's full name followed by an impressive array of letters. The small lady knocked almost reverently, and they both waited for several seconds before a voice commanded, "Come." Shadow took a deep breath, as the lady opened the door to announce him, before scuttling back to her desk.

Stather's room was about three times the size of the outer office with a large window overlooking Kings Square and the Minster. The archaeologist was reading at his desk and didn't bother to look up. He held one finger in the air.

"I'll be with you in one moment, Chief Inspector."

Shadow ignored him. He walked over and slapped a copy of the petition down on the desk in front of him. "That is your signature isn't it, Dr Stather?"

Stather looked up startled and then down at the petition. "Yes, it is but excuse me, Chief Inspector, what does this have to do with finding Emma Harrison in Museum Gardens?" he asked, with a barely disguised flicker of irritation.

"Nothing at all, Dr Stather. Actually, I'm here in relation to a more recent death. That of Miss Ruth Brooke?"

Stather paled visibly. He sank back into his chair and slowly removed his reading glasses. Shadow watched him. Either he was a very good actor, or he really hadn't heard about Ruth.

"I understand you were once in a relationship with her?" Shadow continued. Stather nodded his head slowly, looking down as he cleaned his glasses, so Shadow couldn't see his expression. When he finally spoke, he picked his words carefully.

"I wouldn't call it a relationship exactly. We stepped out together a few times, but that was many years ago. Poor Ruth."

"It was thirty-two years ago to be exact, when she had a teaching position here in York. Have you seen her since?"

Stather shook his head and without looking up. "No, no I haven't. Poor Ruth," he repeated. "How did she die?"

"She was poisoned. Not far from here."

Stather looked up then. "She was in York?" he stammered, unconvincingly.

Shadow raised an eyebrow. "Dr Stather, I really think it would be better if you started telling me the truth. You were seen speaking to her, down by the river, on the day she died."

"Who says so?" he asked, suddenly defensive and there was real panic in his eyes.

"I do," replied Shadow, finally taking a seat as he watched the archaeologist's shoulders gradually droop. "When did you realise she had returned to the city?"

Stather twisted round in his chair to look out of the window, across the square and down Petergate.

"Just a few days ago. I must have walked past her a hundred times without realising. I could almost see where she had made her home from here." He paused, as if lost in his thoughts. "I only realised it was her when I heard her speaking one day. She was reciting poetry—Wordsworth, I think. I recognised her voice immediately, but I could hardly believe it was her. She looked so different. So tired and dishevelled. She had always been a neat and tidy sort of a girl."

"Did she recognise you?" asked Shadow.

Stather shook his head. "I don't think so, but I was too much of a coward to approach her in a public place. I wanted to wait until she alone. Then I saw her down by the river. It was quite by chance, Chief Inspector, you must believe me."

Shadow noted his voice was almost pleading. The pomposity and air of superiority had totally disappeared, as he continued.

"I tried to tell her about the body that had been found. You see it had already occurred to me that it might be Emma. The whole thing seemed too much of a coincidence for it not to be."

Shadow resisted the temptation to interrupt; he'd learnt long ago not to stop a witness if they were talking willingly. Instead he let Stather continue.

"Ruth always blamed herself for the girl disappearing. She was meant to be watching over them, but she was with me instead. In the statement she gave to the police, she said she heard a splash; in actual fact, she was acting as my lookout instead of supervising the girls. She was so upset and anxious about lying, she had a breakdown and left the city soon afterwards.

"When I approached her, I tried to talk to her, to explain that she shouldn't have blamed herself for what happened, but she didn't want to listen. She even covered her ears at one point and just kept saying 'She was there all the time' over and over. Then she started on with her poetry again and I'm afraid that's when I gave up. That was the last time I saw her, I swear."

"Do you mind telling me where you were on Tuesday evening, Dr Stather?"

The archaeologist looked perplexed for a second, then his

face broke into a relieved smile.

"Yes certainly. I was here working until half past six. My secretary was here too. I then went to meet some associates for supper, as I do every Tuesday, before we take part in a local pub quiz."

Shadow raised an eyebrow, but otherwise didn't react to this news.

"Would that be the quiz at The Snickel Side Inn?"

"Yes," replied Stather, in surprise. "How did you know?"

"Just a guess. Can you tell me what happened the day Emma disappeared?"

Stather took a deep breath, as if trying to compose himself. "Ruth and I had been seeing each other for a little while, but she didn't have much free time away from the college, so she volunteered to accompany the girls to rowing practice, so we could arrange to meet in Museum Gardens. Susie and Emma were both sensible, intelligent girls, almost eighteen. We didn't think they would come to any harm." Stather paused and began fiddling with his glasses again.

"If I'm to be completely honest with you, Chief Inspector, then I should explain that as much as I liked Ruth, I did have another reason for wanting to meet her when she was down at the boat shed. You see I was young and ambitious. I had just started working here, and I was keen to make my mark, so to speak. We had begun work excavating a small area around the Hospitium. I was convinced there was a tunnel leading down to the boat shed. I'd spent hours poring over old maps and it was going to be part of my thesis.

However, my superiors here were quite dismissive of the idea and they refused to ask St John's for permission for me to access the boathouse."

"So, Ruth was your only way in?" Shadow asked. He could picture it. The young, shy, romantic Ruth flattered by the attention of the clever, confident young man, not wanting to refuse him.

"Yes, she didn't mind. She said she was happy to help. I knew exactly where to look, but the only time I could do it was when the other archaeologists weren't there, so a Saturday morning was perfect. In the boathouse there was a basement beneath the changing rooms. It was used as a sort of storeroom. It had a wooden floor, so I simply prised up a couple of boards and there was the tunnel exactly as I knew it would be. Ruth and I went through as far as we could trying to find where it ended at the Hospitium, but part of the tunnel had collapsed and Ruth was claustrophobic, so it was quite difficult.

"On the day Emma died, we decided to try from the Hospitium end. As I said it was early on Saturday so nobody else was working, but to make sure I wasn't disturbed Ruth kept watch on the balcony."

"Why were the girls at school on a Saturday morning?"

"All the independent schools have Saturday morning school, often for sports practice or other activities. Although I suspect the real reason is to keep the boarding pupils occupied."

Shadow nodded as he recalled his own school days.

"Why did you lie to us about the tunnel on the night we found Emma?"

"I panicked. My thesis was published within a year of Emma disappearing. If you started to ask questions and found out the tunnel had never been officially excavated, my professional reputation would be in tatters. I came up with a story loosely based on the truth, in the hope you may accept it."

Shadow was amazed such an intelligent man could be so naïve. Perhaps he was just used to never having his opinions or authority questioned. There was something else Stather had said that bothered him though.

"So, Susie and Emma knew what you were doing?" he asked.

"Oh yes. Emma, in particular, seemed quite interested." He sighed. "She was such a bright girl and breathtakingly beautiful."

"Did anyone else know?"

"Possibly, I'm not sure. I told them it was meant to be a secret, but they were young, and it was such a long time ago. I do know that Ruth spoke to someone that weekend. I'm not sure if it was a parent or another member of staff, but they advised her against changing her statement. They used words like perjury and wasting police time. It frightened her and I think it was probably an added factor in her break-down."

Shadow thought for a moment. It was indeed many years ago, but he felt what he had been told was more relevant than ever. He remembered what George had told him about the original investigation. There were plenty of characters who could have influenced Ruth. Luke Carrington's father or the headmaster, perhaps Miss Hall or maybe even Shadow's predecessor, Grunwell. He stood up slowly and turned to go. Stather was staring out of the window once more as if lost on his own world. Shadow paused.

"By the way, when did you hear the body we found was definitely Emma? Did you watch the news last night?"

"No, Chief Inspector, I never watch television. Her brother Oliver told me. He actually came up here to thank me. You see, he realised it was thanks to our excavation that she was found."

SHADOW DESCENDED THE stairs from Stather's office wearily. Oliver had told Stather about Emma, but not Ruth. Did that mean he didn't know Stather had been in a relationship with her? As for Stather being at The Snickel Side Inn on Tuesday, would he really have admitted to being next to where Norman died so readily, if he was guilty? The feeling of claustrophobia was beginning to overwhelm him again. He almost felt a stranger in his home city. It was as if by investigating these deaths he'd entered another place where every victim, witness and suspect were connected. Was that why he still had the nagging feeling that Emma was connected to these recent murders?

He stepped out on to Shambles to find his way blocked by the large, menacing figure of Eric Morrison. He doubted it was a coincidence.

"Are you waiting to speak with me, Mr Morrison?"

"Too right I am. You've got a cheek bothering Mandy when she's at work." His voice loud enough to cause the tour party, plugged into their commentary headphones, to stop and stare. Shadow smiled and nodded at them.

"I am investigating several murders, Mr Morrison," he replied calmly.

"Yeh, murders you tried to pin on me."

"Nobody was trying to pin anything on you, we simply needed to confirm your whereabouts. After all you had been heard using threatening language towards the homeless community."

"Homeless community huh." Eric almost spat out the words. "What a load of politically correct rubbish. At least I'm honest. I say what I think."

"I understand you have an alibi, Mr Morrison."

"That's right, so why don't you pick on somebody else?"

"Any suggestions?"

The two men were practically pinned together in the doorway now, as a large Chinese tour party slowly made their way down the street. It was another hot day. Shadow was close enough to Eric to see the beads of sweat on his upper lip and smell stale cigarettes on his breath when he spoke.

"If I were you, I'd start with Luke Carrington. All those young vulnerable girls turning up at The Haven. Fay thought he was God's gift. What if something happened with her, but he needed to keep her quiet? He couldn't have anything spoiling the cushy life he's got with Susie."

Shadow recalled how Ted had spoken about Luke.

"I get the feeling you and Ted aren't big fans of Mr Carrington."

Eric's lip curled up into a snarl. "You wouldn't be either if you were Ted. Carrington cost him his job."

"What job was that?" Shadow was genuinely surprised. Ted had been working at the bar for as long as he could remember.

"Back in the day, Ted used to be a roadie. He toured all over the world with some big names. For a while he worked as a roadie for Susie too, until Carrington senior fired him. Said he had been supplying dope to Susie and Luke, when really it was the other way around. Poor old Ted got done for supplying, while precious little Luke only got a caution for possession. He's always had things too easy. First Daddy took care of everything, now Susie's the one he sponges off."

"Did Susie know about Luke and Ted?"

"Of course she did, but all she has ever cared about is Luke. She has worshipped him since they were kids. God knows why. Why else do you think she let Luke's dad be her manager when she could have had one of the big boys from London? It was all about Luke. Ted couldn't understand it. Nobody could."

CHAPTER EIGHT

Down 8 (3 letters)
Rowing at home makes almost half board a better idea

AFTER ERIC HAD finished having his say and the tour party had passed by, Shadow managed to extract himself from the crowds on Shambles. He reasoned his day was unlikely to improve, so with a sense of resignation, he headed across to Ted's bar. He found Ted, wearing dark sunglasses, leaning against the wall outside and puffing on a cigarette. He didn't bother to hide his displeasure in seeing Shadow.

"Not you again! I told that Chinese lad already, Eric was here all night."

"Yes, but you forgot to tell him about the dope you've been selling from here."

Ted gave Shadow a contemptuous look and slowly shook his head.

"Not me, I haven't been selling anything but booze."

"No, you've been getting other people to do your dirty work. Others who don't have a record, like Fay Lawton. Is that why you got rid of her, because she didn't want to work for you anymore?"

Ted threw his cigarette to the ground in disgust. He used his now unemployed fingers to point accusingly at Shadow.

"Fay has nothing to do with me and I've never touched dope. Why don't you go and bother someone else?"

"Someone else like Luke Carrington?"

"Why not? The bloke's a psycho. He tried slashing his wrist when Ollie Harrison told him you'd dug up his old girlfriend. Not that he could even get that right! He's a nutter, and whoever's got it in for the poor sods sleeping out on the streets is a nutter. So, go find him and stop wasting my time."

Ted turned on his heel and stalked back into the bar. Shadow gave a heavy sigh. He had at least provoked Ted enough to learn a little more. He left Colliergate and walked down St Andrewgate, passing the entrance to Granary Court. As he did so, he glanced up to Luke and Susie's penthouse. It occurred to him that perhaps he should have investigated what was being grown in the greenhouse on the balcony. What if old habits died hard for Luke, and he was still involved with supplying dope? He certainly didn't seem to have any other way of earning an income. Surely nobody ever bought those terrible paintings.

Eric seemed adamant that Susie's past earnings were enough to support them both, but he also seemed to think drugs were behind the murders. Maybe he was right. As for Ted letting him know Luke's injury was self-inflicted, was that the truth? If it was, how did Susie feel? She had seemed calm enough when he'd mentioned it. And was he imagining it or did Eric and Ted seem to be working as a double act? Both had been eager to point the finger at Luke.

With so much new information racing through his head, Shadow decided to pay another visit to Museum Gardens. He hadn't been back there since the night they found Emma. It was less than seventy-two hours ago, but so much had happened it felt far longer. He walked down Deansgate and paused to watch the children of The Minster School dancing around a maypole. Proud parents and grandparents smiled and clapped. Shadow watched the little boys and girls skip around each other as the multi-coloured ribbons twisted farther and farther down the pole. They reminded him of the case. The more he investigated, the more the suspects, victims and witnesses appeared to become intertwined. All their lives weaving in and out of each other's.

He moved on. He'd never been very fond of children, even when he was one.

ON SUCH A warm, sunny afternoon the Museum Gardens were crowded. Teenagers lolled on the grass, self-consciously smoking cigarettes. Office workers, without their jackets, ate sandwiches, as they grabbed a breath of fresh air. Young mothers held the hands of toddlers, who squealed in delight as some of the most well-fed squirrels in the country tamely came running for handfuls of nuts. Shadow recalled doing the same when he was a little boy. It was one of his few happy childhood memories. Although his mother had loved him in her own way, after his father had died when he was just an infant, she had either been too anxious, tired or preoccupied to show him much affection.

She had always made sure he had clean clothes and was well fed, but there had never been the hugs at the primary school gate or the bedtime stories he knew his classmates enjoyed. She had made no comment when his teacher had encouraged him to sit a scholarship exam to a boarding school in Hampshire. Then when he was successful and disappeared down south for weeks at a time, she had only sent a letter each month, largely about the weather and always signed simply 'from Mum.'

He couldn't help envying the other boys, who seemed to receive daily letters and parcels of food from home or surprise weekend visits from their proud fathers and adoring mothers. He knew she worked long hours at the chocolate factory, but he often returned at the end of term, to find there was nobody waiting for him on the station platform. Over time he had come to understand how difficult it must have been to raise a child alone, but still, it had been a lonely childhood for a little boy.

The one quiet area of the gardens was between the Hospitium and the old boat shed. Bright yellow police tape ran between the two buildings and signs asking the public for information regarding Emma's death were dotted around. The two uniformed officers who were meant to be on duty quickly sprang to their feet and replaced their helmets when they saw Shadow duck under the tape.

"Any news?" he asked. The older of the two officers shook his head.

"Not really, sir. A few people have stopped to ask us what's going on, oh and there was someone hanging around the boathouse first thing when we came on duty. He took off when we called out to ask him what he was doing here. A tall, skinny bloke with a ponytail."

"All right, thank you, Constable."

Shadow took their place on the newly vacated bench and tried to imagine what it must have been like on the day Emma disappeared, thirty-two years ago. All those cases of unrequited love—Oliver for Susie, Susie for Luke, and Ruth for Stather—he wondered if there was anyone he'd missed out. Of those only Susie and Luke had gone on to become a couple. Shadow thought theirs was a strange relationship. He knew what it was like to love somebody so much you would do anything to make them happy, but there needed to be a balance.

Susie obviously adored Luke, but when Luke spoke affectionately about Susie, it was about what she did for him, not the woman herself. He also sensed their relationship wasn't always based on honesty. If the truth would cause distress it was simply swept away or twisted into something else. He wasn't surprised to hear Luke had been seen hanging about the boathouse. He seemed incapable of leaving the past behind.

With a sigh, Shadow stood up and wandered up and down between the boathouse and the Hospitium. The original building work had come to a halt, but the medieval tunnel down to the river was now fully exposed. If Emma had been killed away from the boathouse could her killer have hidden her body in the tunnel? Would they have accessed it from the Hospitium end or from the boathouse? Or could she have arranged to meet someone in the tunnel and been killed there? Stather thought his work back then was a secret, but how many others knew about it? Shadow wasn't sure, but he could only imagine how frustrated Stather must be not to be involved in this excavation.

He turned and began to climb the steps up to the balcony of the Hospitium, where Ruth had stood as lookout. From there he had a wonderful view of the Museum Gardens, right down to the river. On such a beautiful day it was almost impossible to believe that on an equally beautiful day, a young girl had lost her life here. As he looked around, a flash of pink by the Marygate entrance gate caught his eye. His first thought was of Cristina from the day before, when she was wearing the bright pink top down by the river. However, as he strained his eyes, he realised it was Jess, the young girl from The Haven with her bright pink hair. She was talking and laughing with Luke Carrington. They hugged and Luke turned back towards Marygate, while Jess began walking through the gardens.

The late afternoon sun was now becoming unbearably hot for the chief inspector, who was still wearing his wax jacket, but as quickly as he could, he made his way back down the balcony steps. Jess was just approaching the Hospitium.

"Hello, Jess," Shadow called out, trying not to sound breathless. Jess smiled weakly.

"Hi, Chief Inspector Shadow."

"How are you? How's everything at The Haven?"

Jess shrugged and began chewing the corner of her thumb.

"A bit weird still. Everyone is pretty upset, but Susie is holding it all together."

"Yes, she seems to be very good at that. Is Luke the same?"

Jess's face brightened. "Oh, Luke's great too, but he's a lot more intense than Susie. He reacts more, you know, more ups and downs."

"Like when Susie bought the wrong vodka for his birthday?"

Jess stopped chewing her nail and gave a little laugh. "I don't know why he got so upset. It was all so stupid, besides Holy Cow doesn't even taste that nice."

"You've tried it?" Shadow asked. He was sure none of the

bottles Susie had shown him had been opened.

Jess ran her fingers through her hair. "Yeh, on a nightmare blind date. He was into really cringy old music and bought me expensive vodka to show off. I mean who our age goes to Ted's Bar?"

"Ted's Bar was selling Holy Cow?" Shadow tried to keep his voice even.

"I know right? It's the kind of place where you expect the wine to come out of a box."

"Sorry, when was this, Jess?"

"About a month ago. Look, sorry, Chief Inspector, but I have to go. I'm on my way to enrol in a college course. Susie thinks it will be good for me."

"Yes, certainly. Nice to talk to you again, Jess."

Shadow watched her hurry off past a group of giggling schoolgirls, but in his head all he could hear was the smash of glass, as Cristina emptied a box into the recycling bin. As he headed back towards the Museum Garden gates, a familiar pungent smell filled his nostrils. He glanced down and spotted an equally familiar figure sprawled across the grass. There was a large spliff smouldering between his fingers and his Tilley hat was covering his face. Byron's devotion to plant-based products obviously extended beyond food.

Shadow reached into his pocket and pulled out his phone. Then for the first time since they had started working together, he called his sergeant.

"Chief, is that you? Is everything all right?" Jimmy asked

as soon as he answered. He sounded worried.

"Yes, why?" replied Shadow.

"You're calling me on your mobile."

"I know," sighed Shadow in exasperation. His sergeant's habit of stating the obvious could be extremely irritating. "Now stop asking stupid questions and tell me when the bins are emptied in the city centre."

"The bins," echoed Jimmy, "well it depends, Chief. You see the grey bins, which hold the regular household waste, they are collected on a Monday, but then there are the blue recycling bins. There's the one for cardboard and…"

"The glass one," interrupted Shadow, wishing he'd been granted the gift of patience.

"Oh, that's Friday, so tomorrow morning."

"In that case, get hold of forensics and meet me outside Ted's bar, as soon as possible." And with that he hung up.

SHADOW WAS THE first to arrive at Ted's. A small group of customers were standing outside smoking and laughing. He waited for them to go back inside, then hurried past the window and around the corner, into the alley where the bins were kept. Hoping nobody had seen him, he lifted the lid of the glass recycling bin and recoiled as he was struck by an overwhelming smell of vodka. He peered inside. The bin was almost full of empty green wine bottles and smaller brown beer ones, but near the bottom it was possible to make out some tiny clear glass bottles with the now-familiar Holy Cow label. Judging by the smell they certainly hadn't been empty when they were deposited there.

At that moment, there was the sound of running feet and Jimmy appeared at the entrance to the alleyway. "I got here as soon as I could, Chief," he said, trying to catch his breath. "Forensics are stuck on the other side of the city, but they said they would get here ASAP."

Shadow pointed inside to the contents of the bin. "When they get here, tell them the mini bottles of Holy Cow are at the bottom. Most are smashed, but I think some are still in one piece. I want to know how many were thrown out and if what was inside them was pure Holy Cow."

Shadow glanced at his watch. It was hours since he'd last eaten—no wonder his stomach was growling. Fortunately, on his way back to *Florence* he passed Little Sicily, another of his favourite Italian restaurants. A sudden screech of tyres in the street outside told him forensics had arrived.

"Whatever they find, it's not going to be enough to arrest Ted, but interview him under caution and see what you can get out of him," he instructed his sergeant.

"Where are you going, sir?" asked Jimmy, as Shadow stalked away.

"To get something to eat."

For once, Shadow wasn't only thinking of his stomach. If Jimmy wanted his career in CID to progress, he was going to have to get used to confronting tough nuts like Ted on his own. Not every interview he conducted would be sipping lemonade with the likes of Susie Slater. Shadow knew perfectly well Ted wouldn't give anything away. He was an old hand when it came to dealing with the police and would know immediately they didn't have the evidence, or he would be under arrest and in a cell. Still, the best way for Jimmy to learn how to handle these situations was through experience.

LATER THAT EVENING, as the sun began to fall, the temperature showed no sign of doing the same. It was stuffy on board *Florence*. Shadow left the cabin door open as he prepared an evening snack of Wensleydale and crackers. He was really still quite full after his supper at Little Sicily, but the cheese would nicely help the bottle of Valpolicella he'd opened to go down. Ella Fitzgerald's soothing voice poured out of the stereo speakers, as he settled down on the sofa.

On the table in front of him was his phone. Jimmy had attempted unsuccessfully to call him while he was eating and so had resorted to sending a long string of text messages instead. It was as Shadow had expected. Forensics had said twenty full miniature bottles had been put in the bin. The vodka was definitely Holy Cow and had not been contaminated. When Jimmy had attempted to question him, Ted's response had been an unwavering 'no comment.'

Shadow took a sip of wine. If Ted was linked to the murders, they were going to have to start look elsewhere for a breakthrough.

SITTING ALONGSIDE SHADOW'S phone were the two case folders he had brought home with him. George would be horrified if he knew any of his precious files were this close to open water. Shadow opened Emma's folder first and took out her photo. He still found it almost impossible to reconcile the beautiful, smiling girl, so full of promise, with the skeleton they found in an ancient, damp tunnel. Of course, it wasn't only her life that ended that day. Her parents, Oliver, Luke and even Ruth, none of them had fully recovered, so many other lives damaged. Suddenly, his thoughts were interrupted as outside the geese started honking loudly again.

"For crying out loud," muttered Shadow under his breath. He put the photographs down and went to close the door. He'd rather bake than be deafened. He put his head out of the door to see what the geese were complaining about. He looked across the deck, then froze. Walking down the towpath towards him was Cristina and the tall, stocky, bald man he had seen her with the day before when he was at The King's Head. He quickly ducked back inside as they walked by. He could hear them talking, but it was in an Eastern European language he couldn't understand.

When they had passed by, Shadow stuck his head out again and watched them. They walked further down the path for a couple of minutes then stopped and sat down together on the riverbank. The man had his arm around her shoulder and their conversation looked intense, but Shadow didn't think they were romantically involved. He went back to the galley to collect his wine and cheese, then returned to the deck to sit and watch.

It was dusk and the light was fading, although the rising moon was full and bright. Shadow wasn't concerned they would notice him—they seemed far too engrossed in each other, and thanks to Cristina's bright blonde hair there was no danger he'd lose sight of them. He pondered that with their choice of hair colour, neither Cristina nor Jess were ever likely to go unnoticed.

Shadow waited, ate his cheese and sipped his wine. The air was beginning to cool, and in the distance the Minster bells struck nine. A group of loud, drunken racegoers shouted and laughed as they crossed Skeldergate Bridge. A large electric-blue hat was snatched off one girl's head and thrown into the water, accompanied by shrieks and squeals, but nobody came down to retrieve it. Another hour passed. Suddenly the geese began to honk angrily again. They really were better than any pack of guard dogs.

Shadow strained his eyes and sure enough a small motorboat was heading up the river. He turned to see Cristina and her companion were now on their feet. The man raised his hand to greet the boat. Shadow went back inside to retrieve his binoculars. When he looked again, the boat was now turning towards the riverbank and its engine was switched off. In the moonlight, Shadow could just make out the name *Humber Jack*.

A man shouted from the boat in a foreign language and threw a rope across. It was caught by Cristina's companion, who then pulled the boat towards him. There was a soft bump as the boat touched the riverbank. Cristina and the man she was with embraced briefly, then he jumped on the boat and with his foot pushed it away from the bank. The engine was switched on again and the boat turned and headed back from where it had come. Cristina waved briefly, then stood motionless, as she watched the boat disappear into the night. Finally, when she was sure it had gone, she turned and retraced her steps along the towpath towards Shadow. He waited until she was level with him.

"Good evening, Cristina," he said quietly. She spun round in surprise, then froze when she saw him. "It's late to be out. Doesn't Ted need you at the bar tonight? I thought you would want to be with him, especially after my sergeant paid him a visit earlier."

Cristina stared at him angrily, with her hands on her hips. "What do you want?" she asked, defensively.

"Just to talk. Why don't you come aboard?" he replied,

calmly. He stood up and offered her his hand. She seemed to weigh up her options for a moment, then with a small shrug, took his hand and stepped on board. She sat down and looked around.

"This is a strange place for a policeman to live. Do you live here alone?"

"Yes."

"Have you always?"

"No."

Cristina nodded and studied him with eyes that were far older than her years. Shadow imagined working in Ted's bar, she was used to listening to the woes of lonely middle-aged men. He excused himself and disappeared into the galley, returning with another wine glass. He poured her a drink before topping up his own glass.

"So, what do you want to talk about?" she asked, warily.

"Two nights ago, I saw you with Mandy Morrison in her boutique."

Cristina threw her head back and laughed. "That's what you want to talk to me about? Trying dresses on after hours?"

"I thought it seemed strange, that's all."

"Mandy owed me money. I modelled for her at a fashion show a few months ago and she didn't pay me. She wanted to give me a dress instead of cash."

"Is that usual?"

"No, but I don't think Mandy's business is doing as well

as she wants everybody to think. The dress she wanted to give me was very nice, but it was also a size eight. Don't think I am unkind Mr Shadow, but not many of the ladies who are Mandy's usual customers are a size eight. I doubt she would have been able to sell it anyway."

"So, you didn't take it."

"No." Cristina paused and took a long sip of her wine. "We came to another arrangement."

"In your opinion, the fashion show wasn't a success?" Shadow continued to probe.

Cristina wrinkled her nose and shook her head. "No, I think it cost her more to put it on than she got in sales. She even tried to get Susie Slater to be one of the models. Mandy thought a famous name would bring in more people. She said she would drop the petition about the soup kitchen if she did, but it wasn't Susie's thing. Some of the clothes were real fur and Susie didn't like it. She said she and Luke hated cruelty to animals and would not help Mandy."

"So, the fashion show lost money and Mandy tried to recoup some, by selling the vodka on to Ted?"

"I don't know this word recoup." Cristina frowned. "But Ted bought the vodka for half price. When your policemen telephoned about it, he told me to get rid of it all."

As Shadow was listening to her, he recalled the commotion the geese were making on the night he couldn't sleep. Perhaps it hadn't just been the rain that had excited them. He decided to take a chance.

"And after you left Mandy, without the dress, you came down here to the river." He framed it as a statement, not a question.

Cristina, who had begun to relax a little, stiffened suddenly. She began to fiddle with the stem of her glass, and he could see she was trying to decide whether to tell him the truth or not. With a small sigh, she finally gave a slight nod.

"With your companion?" Shadow pressed.

Cristina took another sip of wine, then began to rummage through her vast handbag. It was adorned with a famous designer's logo, but Shadow suspected it was probably a fake. Cristina finally located her cigarettes and lighter.

"Do you mind?" she asked. Shadow shook his head. He picked up the lighter and held the flame steady. She bent her head forward to ignite the cigarette, clamped firmly between her red lips. Then she leaned back and inhaled deeply, before slowly blowing out a long plume of smoke.

"He is my brother, Marius," she finally, admitted. "We came over here together. I met Ted and moved here, and Marius got a job working on some building sites in Hull, but then he broke his arm and couldn't work. He got behind with his rent. He wanted to go home, but couldn't afford to. I tried to help, but he got in with a bad crowd. Albanians!" She almost spat out the last word.

"You aren't Albanians too?"

"No!" She looked offended. "We are Romanians, Chief Inspector! They said they would give him the money to get home, but they wanted him to help first move drugs into York. They had no contacts here, but they knew Marius had me."

"So, two nights ago you met the boat and collected the last delivery?"

"No, it was too dangerous. After all the rain, the current was too strong. The boat headed back, and we had to drive to Hull."

"By we, you mean Eric Morrison?"

Cristina took another long drag on her cigarette. "Yes, he'd already been drinking when we went back to the bar, but Ted talked him into it. He said he owed him a favour because of the vodka, and I told him I would forget about the money Mandy owed me, so he said he would."

"So, Ted knew about all of this? He was involved too?"

"No." She shook her head firmly. "Absolutely not. He knew nothing until that night. He was upset with me and angry with Marius. He said no decent brother would drag his sister into dealing drugs."

For once Shadow was inclined to agree with Ted. He now understood why Ted and Eric were so keen to deflect attention away from themselves and were encouraging Shadow to investigate Luke instead. With Ted's previous conviction, he really couldn't afford to be linked to any drug deals.

"But, when we took Eric in for questioning, Ted had to back up Eric's alibi?" he asked.

Cristina nodded. "Yes. For my sake. Please believe me. Ted is very good to me. I don't want to bring him any more trouble."

Shadow felt as though some pieces of this particular part of the puzzle were finally fitting together.

"It's all right, I do believe that night was the only time Eric and Ted were involved. However, you did get Ryan to help with the distribution?"

Cristina nodded again. Her lips began to tremble and when she spoke there was a catch in her voice. "He knew everyone on the streets who were users. That was what caused the argument between him and Fay the night she died. Fay was a good girl. What happened—it was my fault. If she hadn't argued with Ryan, maybe she would still be here." A tear rolled down Cristina's cheek. She quickly brushed it away with the back of her hand. "Am I going to be arrested, Chief Inspector?"

"That depends. Is tonight the end of it?"

"Yes, this time tomorrow Marius will be back home. He's taking the 8am ferry. The Albanians know you are watching Ted and the bar now, so Marius being here is too big a risk."

"Then I don't think we need to take this any further. Is the dope all gone?"

Cristina picked up her handbag and began rummaging through again. She pulled out about a dozen small bags of the stuff and placed them on the seat next to Shadow.

"This is all that's left. Marius had it; he just gave it to me. He didn't want to be caught with it. You think I should flush it down the toilet or throw it in the river?"

Shadow had a sudden vision of his greedy neighbours eating whatever ended up in the river. The last thing he needed was stoned geese staggering about the place. Then, remembering something he'd seen in Fay's folder, he scooped up the bags.

"No, I want you to donate it to a charitable cause."

Cristina looked confused but shrugged and didn't argue. She knocked back the last of her wine, stood up a little unsteadily and tossed the end of her cigarette into the water.

"Allow me to walk you home?" Shadow offered, self-consciously. It was a long time since he had walked an attractive young lady home.

"No thank you, Chief Inspector. This is a safer city than most. I'll be okay and I don't think Ted would like it." She quickly leaned forward and brushed her lips against Shadow's cheek.

Shadow was relieved it was dark and she couldn't see him blush. He took her hand and helped her ashore. As he did, he noticed several scars near her knuckles.

"You've hurt your hand," he observed.

"Cuts and burns from when I was making moussaka yesterday. I think I must have been distracted with all this."

She gave a small smile then turned and walked away. Shadow watched her go and his eyes followed her across the bridge, where she paused briefly. There was a flicker of a flame as she lit another cigarette, before moving on.

He suddenly had an uncomfortable feeling that tonight's meeting may not have been unplanned. He thought back to how Cristina had made sure he and Jimmy had witnessed her at the recycling bin, noisily dumping the bottles, when they first visited Ted. She had admitted that by investigating the bar he had inadvertently made it possible for her brother to return home. As he watched her progress, he shook his head. Just when he thought things were becoming clearer, they had suddenly clouded again. Finally, she was out of sight, the geese were quiet, and he could go to bed.

NOT THAT HE could sleep. Once again thoughts kept drifting through his head, though this time they weren't about dead bodies or drug deals. He was remembering the last evening he'd sat outside on the boat, sharing a bottle of wine with a beautiful young girl, with the sound of water lapping and the smell of cigarette smoke in the air. It was over twenty years ago now. He and Luisa had barely had two years together, but they had been the happiest time he'd known.

She'd left Italy to study at the London Business School, close to Regent's Park. One day, she was walking by the canal and had passed, as he was repainting *Florence*. She had laughed and told him he should rename the boat *Lecce*, after her home city, as it was far more beautiful than Florence. Shadow couldn't argue, as he'd never been to Italy or anywhere else abroad. Luisa had teased him about that. She'd teased him about lots of things, like his old-fashioned taste in music and the fact he'd only ever eaten spaghetti out of a tin until he'd met her.

The meals she created for them in the tiny galley had been incredible. She'd presented him with ingredients and dishes he'd never even heard of. They had planned to go to Italy together. They were going to tour round the country when she had finished her degree and he had completed his exams to be promoted to sergeant, but it wasn't to be. One wet, dark December evening, when Luisa was on her way home, a drunk driver had swerved across the road and hit her. After she'd gone, he knew he couldn't stay in London. He had asked to be transferred back up north and had never returned to the capital.

Restlessly, he turned his head on the pillow. Her photo was on the locker by his bed. She was wearing a white summer dress and was laughing as she sat on the roof of the boat. He could remember the day that photo was taken. Dean Martin was playing in the background and Luisa had been trying to teach him the words to 'Volare.' Now, he wished he'd taken more photographs. Apart from the wonderful food and wine she'd introduced him to, they were all he had to remember her.

CHAPTER NINE

Across 6 (4 letters)
This gateau is better if Luca keeps it

E ARLY THE NEXT morning, Shadow stood on Goodram-gate waiting outside The Golden Dragon. He could already feel the warmth from the sun as it rose in the sky. The street was deserted except for a van from the local dairy delivering milk to the various pubs, shops and restaurants. In the distance, he could still see the wilting floral tributes to Fay. As the dairy van rumbled away, Jimmy stepped out of his front door, in shorts and vest, to set off for his morning run. The muffled angry beat of rap music escaped from his headphones as he lunged from side to side, warming up the muscles in his long legs.

He stopped abruptly mid-stretch and looked shocked to see Shadow standing there, holding two large case files. He quickly removed his headphones as Shadow began to briefly recount his conversation with Cristina from the night before and explain his plan.

His sergeant looked worried. "You know if anyone finds out about this, you could get into a lot of trouble, Chief?"

"I thought you'd be pleased we finally know where the drugs came from. You've been convinced that's the link to Fay's death since we started," Shadow reassured him, but Jimmy's face was still troubled. "Look, we see enough of the problems this stuff causes, why not let it do some good for a change?"

Shadow removed a scruffy-looking piece of paper from one of the folders before handing them both over to Jimmy. He knew what would stop his sergeant worrying.

"Jog by the station and put these back in my office, would you? Then when you get to work properly any time after nine, ring the drugs team in Hull. Ask for Inspector Atkinson. Explain to him that you've had an anonymous tip-off about an Albanian gang bringing drugs into York. Tell him to look out for a boat called *Humber Jack*. Marius might be out of the way, but I don't think for one second they'll leave Cristina alone permanently if they think she can offload their drugs for them."

As he expected, Jimmy's expression changed immediately from concern to excitement.

"No problem, Chief," he replied enthusiastically, already heading off down the street.

"Remember not to call Hull until after nine," Shadow called after him. He didn't want anything interfering with Cristina's brother getting away on the ferry. Jimmy briefly turned back and waved in agreement. Shadow watched him jog away and smiled to himself. Jimmy always complained that Hull and Leeds dealt with more exciting cases than their own city. Maybe if this went well, Jimmy might even put in for a transfer.

As well as hardly ever cooking at home, Shadow also preferred to have the bulk of his laundry done elsewhere. *Florence* was equipped with a washing machine and Shadow's old-fashioned sensibilities meant he took care of his socks and underwear himself. However, shirts, trousers and jackets were all taken to a laundry run by Maggie, who he'd known since primary school. She was short, bossy, loud and possibly the city's biggest gossip. She looked up in surprise when he walked through the door.

"Well, well we don't usually see you this early. It's normally Julie who has the pleasure of your company. Although, she did say you were AWOL the other morning. Was it a grisly case that needed solving or have you found somewhere else to go for your bacon and eggs?" she asked, pointedly.

Shadow wearily dumped his bag of washing on the counter. Not for the first time, he thought he should start using the new Turkish laundry on Gillygate instead.

"Who's Julie?"

Maggie began emptying the bag and rolled her eyes in despair. "She's only the woman who serves you breakfast every morning! Honestly! What are you like?"

She quickly began raking through his shirts and trousers, scribbling each item down on the receipt. Shadow watched her. He could remember her being just as efficient back when she was the classroom monitor, collecting the register, wiping the blackboard clean and watering the spider plant on Mrs Frobisher's desk. Her dark, curly hair was always trying to escape from the two tightly plaited pigtails and the cuffs of her navy cardigan were permanently covered in chalked dust from her vigorously banging the blackboard erasers together.

St Chad's had been a large primary school, with many of the classrooms still in prefab buildings from after the war, but Shadow had been happy there. He had certainly been happier charging round the potholed playground playing Bulldog, than at the boarding school in Hampshire he'd been packed off to aged ten. There they'd laughed at his northern accent and sneered at his scholarship. St Chad's had been knocked down ten years ago to make way for a city centre car park. From their class of thirty children, Maggie was the only one he still knew.

Shadow glanced around as she worked. There was a noticeboard next to the counter. One half was filled with the laundry's opening times and terms and conditions. The other half was covered in cards for local businesses. Shadow looked more closely. The cards for Angelique Boutique, Bacchus and Ted's Bar were all neatly pinned there.

"These business cards, do they belong to friends of yours?" he asked.

Maggie paused and glanced at the noticeboard. "Some do, others have been left by my customers. Why?"

"Which is Oliver Harrison?"

"A customer, but probably not a very happy one. He left a jacket with me to be cleaned, covered in blood. It was impossible to shift."

"Did he cut himself?"

"No, he said a friend smashed a glass in his office and he had to help bandage him up."

"What about Mandy Morrison?"

"Oh, I've known Mandy for years. She recommends me to her customers, for any alterations and dry cleaning they want doing. We go out for a drink now and then. It's called being sociable. You should try it some time."

Shadow ignored the dig.

"Do you ever go to Ted's Bar?"

"We used to. Ted always had a bit of a soft spot for Mandy. They used to go dancing together when they were teenagers. Mandy used to have ballroom dancing lessons and Ted would take her to those Northern Soul clubs over in Leeds. They were quite the movers. Then one weekend she went to see her granny in Scarborough, met Eric, and that was that. Like I said, Ted always held a torch for her, and I think she quite liked the attention."

"More unrequited love," Shadow muttered, half to himself. Maggie raised a heavily pencilled eyebrow but continued.

"Well, Eric isn't exactly the world's most romantic husband, but then that blonde foreign piece turned up and put Mandy's nose out of joint. We usually go to The White Swan or Cross Keys now."

Maggie then paused again and held up the shirt Shadow had been wearing the previous evening. There was a small but definite smudge of bright red lipstick. Shadow inwardly cringed, recalling Cristina's brief goodnight kiss.

"You sure there isn't a new lady in your life?" Maggie grinned.

Shadow reached across and tore off his copy of the unfinished receipt and made for the door. "I'm surprised you've never thought of joining the police yourself with those observation skills, Maggie."

"Oh, you're so sharp you'll cut yourself one of these days." She laughed. Her cackling was still ringing in his ears, as he walked down the street.

THE ADDRESS ON the crumpled bit of paper he'd retrieved from the file was in Holgate, a suburb close to the railway station. It was a forty-minute walk from the city centre. Shadow turned on to the correct street and spotted number seven immediately. It was the only house whose front garden had not been covered with tarmac to create more car parking. Instead, its hedge was neatly trimmed, and geraniums were growing in a pot by the front door. He rang the doorbell and waited. It was after nine, so he expected Ross and his mother, who Jimmy had said was a teaching assistant, would have left for work. He pressed the bell again.

A gruff voice from inside shouted, "Hold your horses! I'm coming, I'm coming."

A moment later, there was the sound of chains rattling, keys being turned, and the door finally opened slightly. An old man with grey hair and glasses peered through the two-inch gap at the same height as Shadow's chest.

"Who are you? What do you want?"

Shadow bent down and rummaged through his pockets until he found his warrant card. He held it up to the gap in the door.

"Mr Jones? It's the police, Detective Chief Inspector Shadow."

The door shut abruptly. There were more jangling noises, then it swung open again.

"You'd better come in before you get any curtains twitching," the old man said grudgingly. He was resting heavily on a walking frame. Shadow stepped inside and closed the door behind him. The hallway was clean and tidy, and on the wall going up the stairs were various framed photos of a boy Shadow assumed was Ross, at different ages in school uniform and football kit. The old man eyed him angrily.

"You'd better not be here to cause more trouble for Ross.

He's a good lad. Granted he made a mistake, but he was just trying to help me."

"I know that, and I heard the stuff he got you did help with your condition. So, look on this as a donation," Shadow placed the small bags of dope on the hall table. Ross's grandfather looked at them suspiciously.

"You could be trying to frame Ross for all I know. Why should I trust you?"

Shadow held up his hands. "I'm trusting you too. Those bags have been in my pocket and are covered in my fingerprints. When I leave here, you can call 999 and report me, you can flush the stuff away or if you want, or you can use it to ease your pain. It's up to you."

Without another word Shadow turned and let himself out, leaving the old man staring after him.

WHEN SHADOW ARRIVED back at the station, he wasn't surprised to find Jimmy already outside his office, digital notebook in hand and broad smile on his face. He looked so eager, Shadow was again reminded of his childhood puppy. He had worn exactly the same expression when Shadow used to reach for his lead and shout 'walkies.'

"Did the phone call to Hull go well, Sergeant?" he asked.

"No problems, sir. Inspector Atkinson was very grateful and said he'd keep me posted. Apparently, the guys there have had an Albanian gang on their radar for a while. They've had their vehicles under surveillance, but with no joy. Finding that boat could be a real breakthrough."

Shadow nodded in response. No wonder Jimmy was happy; he'd managed to use the words 'surveillance,' 'radar' and 'breakthrough' in less than a minute. Shadow briefly glanced down at the phone messages that had been stuck on his desk. There was also a thick cream envelope waiting for him. It carried a first-class stamp, and his name and the station address looked like they had been stencilled in. He turned it over. On the back it was marked 'private and confidential.' Shadow slipped it, unopened, into his coat pocket.

He screwed up and binned the messages to call the chief constable and Kevin MacNab. Then he tucked the one from forensics in his pocket. He couldn't face talking to them on an empty stomach, so he turned and headed for the door.

"Are you going out again, sir?" asked Jimmy, trying not to sound dejected.

"I think you know where I'll be, Sergeant."

He was so keen to find some breakfast that he forgot to use the station's side door and instead walked through the main entrance and straight into Kevin MacNab. The journalist had obviously been waiting for him. Shadow cursed under his breath.

"Still no breakthrough Mr Shadow? How many more people will have to die before you catch the killer? Is Emma

Harrison's death linked to the homeless murders?"

Shadow ignored him and stomped past and out across St Helen's Square, as angry with himself as he was with Mac-Nab. Had somebody told him there was a connection between Emma and the others? Shadow shook his head. He knew all the pieces of the jigsaw were there; if only he could make them fit together.

IT WAS LATE in the morning, so there was already a queue forming at Bettys. Reluctantly, Shadow joined the end, behind yet another Chinese tour party. About ten minutes later, just when he was sure his growling stomach must be audible to the whole restaurant, he felt a light tap on his shoulder. It was the dark-haired waitress with the tired eyes, who had appeared behind him.

"If you don't mind not having your normal table, I can find you space downstairs."

Shadow was so hungry, he would happily have eaten out in the street, so he obediently followed her down the curved staircase to the lower dining room. It was decorated in the art deco style and although there were no windows, the wooden walls were ornately carved. He was shown to a corner table.

"Shall I bring you, your usual?" his waitress asked.

"That would be perfect." He shrugged off his coat and

sat down. "Thank you, Julie."

She turned around in surprise and blushed slightly. "You're welcome, John."

Instead of opening his newspaper as usual, he reached behind him, into his coat pocket and dug out the envelope with his stencilled name and address. He opened it carefully. Inside was a single sheet of paper, the same cream colour and good quality as the envelope. He unfolded it. The one line was made up of letters and words torn out of magazines or newspapers. It read:

'Carrington has blood on his Hands.'

Shadow recognised the ornate capital C and the distinctive capital H immediately. They were from *Helping Hand*— the newspaper that Byron sold—and *Corkscrew*—the wine publication he had also seen in Oliver's office. He peered at the sheet more closely. In the top right-hand corner was a small reddish-brown smudge. Shadow stared at the note for a moment longer before quickly folding it away, as Julie approached with his pot of tea.

After his late breakfast, Shadow went to pay his bill at the cash desk in the shop upstairs. On display along with the delicious pastries and cakes, were gift hampers to celebrate various occasions. He pointed to one that included a large teddy with a blue bow tie.

"Can I have that one delivered?"

"Certainly, sir," replied the young cashier in the smart

black uniform. She handed a gift card over and Shadow scribbled George's address on the envelope. Inside he wrote:

'To George and Carol,
Congratulations, Grandma and Grandad.
Best wishes, John.'

WITH HIS HUNGER now sated, Shadow crossed the square and returned to the station. He found Jimmy upstairs, perched on a desk in the incident room. He was staring intently at the two whiteboards on the wall in front of him. On one board were the pictures of the three recent victims: Fay, Ruth and Norman. Alongside them were the possible suspects: Stather, Ted, Eric, Mandy, Cristina, Luke and Susie. On the other board was the old school photo of Emma and those who were in or around Museum Gardens when she disappeared: Susie, Ruth, Oliver, Luke, and Stather. Drawn-on arrows that had been rubbed out then redrawn zigzagged between photos, with notes and annotations scribbled here and there.

Shadow wearily joined his sergeant, but Jimmy's mood was as positive as ever.

"Do you want to hear my latest theory, sir?"

"Do I have a choice?"

"Well, you said when you spoke to Stather, he described Emma as beautiful and bright. Suppose he was secretly in love with her; Ruth realised it and killed Emma in a fit of jealousy. The guilt caused her breakdown and when she came back here someone killed her in revenge. Maybe Luke or Oliver or Stather."

Shadow's forehead wrinkled as he attempted to imagine the delicate Ruth overpowering Emma, the athlete. In the room next door, half a dozen constables were busy writing up witness statements and fielding calls from the public. They had been working hard for days and Shadow knew they were waiting for him to make a breakthrough. The clock on the wall ticked loudly. To Shadow, it sounded like it was mocking him.

"We're getting nowhere fast," he observed, gloomily. "If they have a motive, they also have an alibi."

"Not always watertight though, sir," replied Jimmy. "Stather could have sneaked out of the pub quiz. He's on both of the boards and he's lied to us from the start. He as good as admitted that he knew the body was Emma before we identified her."

"Do you think he could have killed Emma too?"

"Maybe. Emma could have threatened to tell his boss about what he was doing in the Hospitium tunnel."

Shadow leaned back and sighed deeply.

"I don't see it. From what we've been told about Emma, she was a nice girl, certainly not a blackmailer."

"How about Luke and Oliver? They were both in the area. Either of them could've had a row with Emma, maybe killed her by mistake, panicked and hid the body."

"Wouldn't Susie have seen or heard something?"

Jimmy stood up and began pacing between the two boards.

"Well then let's look at the homeless deaths. What about the four who were drinking in Ted's bar? We already know they are happy to cover for each other. They all knew about Marius and the drugs. And we know Mandy had the vodka and the right type of bottle."

"I can't arrest someone just for what they have bought in the past. Susie had the bottles and Holy Cow too remember."

"But what would Susie's motive be? She's spent years taking care of the homeless, why would she want to start bumping them off?"

"Maybe she's been covering for Luke. This arrived for me in this morning's post."

Shadow pulled out the anonymous note from his pocket and unfolded it for Jimmy to read. The sergeant studied it with a frown.

"Shouldn't we pass it to forensics, Chief?"

Shadow shrugged. "Perhaps, but I'm certain we won't find any fingerprints and I already know that the paper and the magazines and newspapers the letters are cut out of all came from Oliver Harrison's office. I would hazard a guess that brownish smudge is Luke Carrington's blood."

"Do you think Oliver was the one who sent it?"

"I think the one who sent it is too clever for their own good."

Without further elaboration, Shadow stuck the note on to one of the whiteboards next to the photo of Oliver and Luke.

Before Jimmy could ask him anything else, there was a knock at the door.

"Come in," shouted Shadow, his frustration showing in his voice more than he meant it to. Sophie tentatively put her head round the door.

"Is this a good time for my report on Norman?" she asked.

"Yes, come in by all means, we could do with break from banging our heads against brick walls," answered Shadow.

Jimmy pulled out a chair for her, as Sophie handed over her report.

"No great surprises, Chief, although having spoken to Donaldson, I would say Norman drank more than the other two victims, almost twice as much in fact. My guess is the poison would have caused him pain, so he knocked back more to try and dull it."

"Poor bugger," muttered Shadow.

Sophie shrugged. "Maybe, but it may have been a blessing in disguise." Both police officers looked at her in surprise; it was unlike Sophie to sound so callous.

"As it turns out, he was in the early stages of liver cancer," she explained, "although I doubt he knew."

"Poor bugger," repeated Shadow, closing the report and pushing it to one side. He was beginning to feel queasy simply talking about it. Sophie pointed to the photographs on the wall behind him.

"That's the rogue's gallery, I take it?"

"Yes, but annoyingly none of them seem to have both motive and opportunity," Shadow grumbled. Then he turned back to the doctor. "While you are here Sophie, can we pick your brains about the cyanide in the vodka? It's not easy to get hold of is it?"

"Not in this country, no, I think you need a licence from the home office, but these days I guess you could buy it over the internet from abroad or on the dark web."

"I could soon find that out, sir?" offered Jimmy. "We would need to look on all the suspects' computers and check their credit card statements. But maybe Cristina and the others involved with the drugs could have found it on the local black market."

Shadow rested his head on his hand. He was thinking back to when they first interviewed Susie as she sat under the cherry tree, in The Haven garden.

"Jake mentioned something about cyanide being in cherry stones—is that right?" he asked.

Sophie nodded. "Yes, and apricot kernels and apple pips. You'd need to ingest quite a few though. I remember we once had a very greedy Labrador, who hoovered up all the cherry stones I spat out." She laughed. "My mother had to rush him off to the vet's. She was livid with me."

Shadow sighed. His life would be much easier if he was looking for someone wanting to bump off the local canine population, but none of the victims had ingested any pips or stones.

"Is it possible to extract the cyanide from the stones or pips?"

Sophie shrugged. "I guess so, if you knew what you were doing, but it wouldn't be easy, and you'd need a fair few apple pips for three murders."

"And it's the wrong time of year. If they wanted to use their home-grown fruit, they would have to have done it at the end of summer last year, and Ruth wasn't here then." Shadow was deep in thought and seemed to be almost talking to himself. Sophie raised a questioning eyebrow at Jimmy, who pointed silently to the photos of Luke and Susie on the board behind them.

"You can buy fruit year-round now, sir," Jimmy suggested.

Shadow shook his head. "I know, I know, but I just can't seem to make it fit. Oh well, you go and see if anyone has been buying something they shouldn't off the internet and I'll go and check if Stather really was at The Snickel Side Inn on Tuesday night."

"Oh, you don't need to go out for that—I can tell you he was," volunteered Sophie. Shadow and Jimmy both turned to look at her. "I'm in a quiz team with a couple of the guys from forensics. We go every week," she explained.

"And you're sure Stather was definitely there all the time on Tuesday?" asked Shadow.

"Oh yes, the archaeology lot take it really seriously. They nearly always win."

"Anything out of the ordinary about that night?"

Sophie paused and thought for a moment. "Not really, a Dutch couple came in absolutely soaked to the skin, but they were good fun and joined in with the quiz too."

"You don't need another member for your team, do you?" asked Jimmy.

Shadow snorted with laughter before Sophie could reply. "What's your specialist subject going to be? Expensive trainers and takeaway coffees?"

Sophie stood up and grinned "You are welcome any time, Jimmy. We're okay on science, sport and geography, but a bit rubbish on music and cookery."

Shadow snorted again and pointed to the whiteboards. "Then you should ask some of our suspects to join you. Apparently, they are a dab hand in the kitchen, churning out moussaka, a three-bean casserole or cassava heavy cake." He laughed, sarcastically.

Sophie stopped abruptly on her way to the door and spun round. "Did you say cassava?"

"Yes, not that I know what it is. Why?"

"It's like a sweet potato. They grow it in Latin America and parts of Africa. You can use it for all sorts of things, even grind it down into a sort of flour, but you need to be careful.

You see you need to wash it thoroughly and you can't eat it raw because it contains high levels of linamarin."

Jimmy and Shadow both looked at her blankly.

"When you eat it, your body turns it into cyanide," she explained.

Shadow slapped his hand against the desk. Finally the pieces of the jigsaw were beginning to fit together.

"I travelled along the Amazon in my gap year and we ate it there," Sophie continued. "I remember the locals saying we should always soak it in water and cook it thoroughly because it could still be poisonous."

Jimmy quickly opened his laptop and began tapping at the keys. "How easy would it be to extract the poison do you think?" he asked Sophie, who was now peering over his shoulder.

"I'm not sure. You would need the right enzyme and probably use the leaves. I think they contain the highest concentration."

Shadow had heard enough. He pulled on his coat and made for the door.

"Where are you going, Chief?" asked Jimmy in surprise.

"Can you still access all the CCTV cameras?" he asked.

His sergeant nodded.

"Then you get ready. I'll call you when I'm in position."

"What on your mobile, sir?"

"Yes, Sergeant, on my mobile. There's no need to look so shocked. Just because I'm not a slave to technology doesn't mean I'm completely incapable."

CHAPTER TEN

Down 4 (6 letters)
By making a blackboard he relates better to pupils

I N LESS THAN ten minutes, Shadow was in Kings Square. It was now the middle of the afternoon and the sun was beating down. The square was full of smiling tourists and busy shoppers. A busker sat on the edge of the old graveyard strumming a guitar badly and a man dressed as a Roman soldier was striding along, handing out leaflets advertising a museum. Teenagers drifted by in shorts and sunglasses. Shadow stood alone in the middle of them all, wearing his old battered wax jacket and looking grimmer than ever.

He thought back to the evening when Norman and Ruth had been killed. Various images flashed through his mind. Norman shuffling along, Byron eating his cake, Susie waving a rubber-gloved hand, Eric and Mandy arguing with Ryan and Kayleigh, and Luke smoking his cigarette. Oliver, Stather, Ted and Cristina were all nearby too. Shadow needed to try and retrace the steps of the killer after they left the square. He fished his phone out of his pocket and made his second call to Jimmy.

"Right, I'm in Kings Square," said Shadow. "Can you see me?"

"Yes, Chief, I've got you. Try and let me know which direction you're going, so I can track you on the screens," replied Jimmy, back at the station.

Shadow began walking down Petergate. There were a few seconds when he disappeared from the screens, then Jimmy found him again. Shadow stopped at the entrance to Lund Court. Since his visit there the other morning, he no longer felt like calling it Mad Alice Lane. Police tape still covered the entrance. Shadow ducked underneath and promptly disappeared from Jimmy's screen. It was cool and dark in the alleyway. Shadow shivered a little. Not only from the drop in temperature, but at the thought of what Ruth must have suffered before she died. Struggling to fight as the poison was being poured down her throat. She was small and weak. It wouldn't have taken long to overpower her.

"I can't see you, Chief." Jimmy's voice from inside his pocket brought him back to reality.

"I think you were right about Ruth and Norman's murderer joining the ghost walk. I'm going to follow the same route, so I'll stay on the line. You let me know when you can see me."

Shadow waited until a large group of students walked by the entrance of the alleyway, then quickly ducked back under the tape and joined them.

"I'm going past Francesco's place now."

"I know, sir," replied Jimmy with a sigh.

Shadow stayed with the tour party as they continued down Petergate, turned right at Minster Gates, through Minster Yard towards Treasurer's House then back again towards the Minster. He kept glancing at his watch to check if the timing would fit with the murders of Ruth and Norman. When he arrived near the West Doors of the Minster, he switched to another tour party that was moving in the opposite direction. He tagged on behind as they went down Petergate until they passed The Snickel Side Inn, when he disappeared from Jimmy's view once again.

"I've lost you, sir."

"I'm in the alley where Norman's body was found. Am I still out of view?"

"Yes, Chief."

"What about now?" Shadow stepped out of the snickelway where Norman died and back on to Petergate.

"Yes, got you, but I'll lose you once you pass under Bootham Bar again."

"That's okay, I'm not going that way. I'm heading to Goodramgate."

"But the ghost walk didn't go that way," said Jimmy sounding confused.

Shadow didn't reply, instead he went back into the narrow passage and walked right through, coming out the other end at Precentor's Court, a private residential street that still housed some members of the Minster's clergy and staff. The main entrance to Precentor's Court was opposite Dean's Park, a quiet garden next to the Minster. He walked through the park and exited on the other side, close to the National Trust Shop, where Jake had spent Monday night.

He understood now how the murderer had avoided appearing on the city's CCTV, both on the night they killed Ruth and Norman, and when they gave Fay the drink that killed her. He was sure now that's what happened. They knew where Fay would be spending the night, paid her a visit and gave her the vodka as a gift. Trusting, naïve Fay no doubt accepted it gratefully, from someone she thought was a friend. That friend had arrived not from Goodramgate, but from the other end of Bedern. Like the other two old snickelways where Ruth and Norman were found, Bedern was also a short cut through to the streets and houses that lay behind.

"Sir? Chief Inspector?" called Jimmy's voice faintly from the phone.

"Can you see me now?" Shadow asked, impatiently, standing in front of Catania and waving his arm in the air.

"Yes, I've found you again, sir. What are you doing?" Jimmy watched as Shadow stepped into Bedern and disappeared from the screens again. There were a few minutes of silence.

"Sir, where are you? I can't see you anywhere?" Jimmy asked. "You are not on any of the screens."

"I'm standing outside Granary Court," replied Shadow.

He turned off his phone and looked up towards the penthouse. It was early evening now and from where he stood it was just possible to see the faint glow from the heaters on the balcony. He now knew exactly what was growing in that greenhouse up there and it wasn't cannabis.

HE WENT TO the door and pressed the bell urgently several times. There was no answer. He didn't wait for Jimmy or bother to tell him where he was going. Angrily, he turned on his heel and headed straight for The Haven. He might be impatient with others when they overlooked things, but he was furious with himself when he made a mistake. Right now, he could kick himself for being so stupid and gullible. The clues had all been there. The greenhouse, the gloves, the bottles. If only he'd checked them properly.

The sun was beginning to set now. Soon the first stars would twinkle in the sky. He recalled the words of Miss Hall: *The stars are always there, but you don't see them when you are dazzled by the sun.*

AS HE HURRIED down Marygate, he remembered The Haven had its own CCTV camera over the front door. He stopped next to the railings and looked down to the basement office window. The light was on, but it was empty. The gate in the railings was heavily padlocked. Pausing to check nobody else was in the street, he clumsily hauled himself over the railings and lowered himself down on to the steps. The broken sash window was still not completely closed. With effort he managed to force it open high enough to get his head in and then wriggle the rest of his body through. He landed on the floor in a heap and staggered to his feet.

The cupboard in the corner was locked, but he located a large pair of scissors on the desk. He slid the open blades between the doors on either side of the lock. Pushing against the handles he applied as much pressure as he could. There was a crash as the lock broke and the doors were flung open. Shadow froze and held his breath. Nothing. If the noise had been heard upstairs, nobody was coming down to investigate.

Shadow knelt down. The box was still there. It had now been resealed with brown tape but hidden at the back of the cupboard was a roll of tape printed with the Bacchus name and logo that must have been used before. Either borrowed or taken from Oliver, by someone he trusted. Shadow tore the box open and began searching through, this time looking at each bottle carefully, as he should have done before.

On the second row, he noticed one bottle had a slightly wrinkled label that wasn't quite straight. He peered more closely, there was a small amount of residual glue on the bottle too. This must have been the label that was removed, photocopied, then stuck back on. He examined the screw cap closely. The seal was broken. Carefully he unscrewed the top and sniffed. There was no smell of vodka. He did the same with two more bottles with broken seals. He guessed they now just contained water, but he wasn't prepared to check himself.

He slipped two of the bottles into his coat pocket, then quietly left the office and headed up to the reception. Jess was behind the desk, engrossed in her book. She jumped when Shadow appeared in front of her.

"Where are they?" he asked, abruptly.

Looking slightly startled, she directed him out into the garden. Shadow ran to the back door, then paused as he took in the scene in front of him.

It was almost idyllic. Luke was sitting on the swing seat with his guitar on the ground next to him. A chicken was clucking contentedly on his lap, as he stroked it with his bandaged hand. Susie was at the far end of the garden dressed in jeans and white shirt, like the first day they'd met. A pair of small pruning shears dangled from her wrist as she tended the wisteria climbing the trellis. Another plant that could be poisonous, thought Shadow. As if sensing his presence, Susie turned round suddenly. Their eyes met for a second, but Shadow couldn't read her expression. Then without saying a word, she jumped on to the top of the chicken house and hauled herself up the trellis.

"Susie where are you going, babe?" shouted Luke. Susie hesitated for a second and glanced back.

"I'm sorry, Luke. I only wanted us to be together," she

called back, then disappeared over the high brick wall. Shadow cursed under his breath. He would never be able to follow her over. Luke stood up, still holding the clucking chicken.

"What does she mean?" he asked, looking at Shadow.

"Susie killed Emma," replied Shadow, abruptly, "and the others."

He left Luke looking stunned and ran back through The Haven as quickly as he could. Running out into the street he headed down towards the river. He turned on to the towpath where the Ouse Cruise Company ticket booth stood. He ran past all the tourist cruisers, motorboats and canoes moored for the night. There was no sign of Susie. He hurried on along the tree-lined path. There was a shout from up on Lendel Bridge. He turned his head to see who it was. As he did, a piece of wood hit him hard in the face and he fell to the ground. The next thing he knew, Jimmy was shaking him and shouting his name.

"Wake up, Chief! Sir can you hear me? Are you okay?"

"What happened?" Shadow managed to whisper, as his sergeant's face slowly came into focus.

"She was waiting behind that tree and smacked you in the face with an oar," explained Jimmy.

"Old habits die hard," muttered Shadow, as he slowly propped himself up on his elbow and gently probed the throbbing lump on his forehead.

"I could see her from the bridge and tried to shout, but

you couldn't hear me."

"How did you know I was down here anyway?"

Jimmy paused for a second, as he chewed his lip nervously.

"I've been tracking your phone, sir," he admitted.

"Well thank God you did. Where is she?"

"I don't know. She'd disappeared when I got here. I've
called uniform for backup. Do you want me to phone you an
ambulance, Chief?"

Shadow slowly sat up and shook his head. Then immediately wished he hadn't as a flash of pain shot through him.
He rummaged through his pocket to find a handkerchief, to
wipe away the blood trickling out of his nose. Just then the
sound of a dog barking loudly caught their attention.
Shadow staggered to his feet, clutching his pounding head.
Jimmy pointed across the river. In the distance, on the
opposite towpath was Jake with a very excitable Missy
running along barking at the shadowy figure of Susie rowing
towards the bridge. She'd taken one of the Ouse Cruise
rowing boats.

"Stop!" yelled Shadow, wincing again at the pain in his
head.

Jake turned round when he heard Shadow, lifted his
hand in recognition, then began to jog along the path trying
to catch up with Susie, as Missy ran ahead.

"Come on, Chief. Down here!" Jimmy was hurrying
along to where the small red motorboats were moored. He

jumped into the nearest one and held out his hand to help Shadow down.

"You wait here, Chief; I'll try and find the keys."

Shadow reached clumsily under the steering wheel, feeling for the wires. He pulled and then fiddled with a couple until the engine purred to life.

"Wow, sir, where did you learn to do that?" asked Jimmy, impressed.

"You don't arrest as many car thieves as I have, without learning about hot wiring. Now get after her." Shadow sank into the passenger seat, as Jimmy revved the engine and set off down the river. Susie had covered a surprisingly long distance and was already nearly at Ouse Bridge, when they caught up with her.

"Susie, give up. We know it was you," Shadow shouted while still clutching the blood-soaked handkerchief to his nose.

She shook her head without turning round. In the distance sirens of the approaching police cars could be heard.

"You can't out-row us," shouted Jimmy.

Now the motorboat was almost alongside her. The waves it was making were causing the little rowing boat to rock dangerously from side to side. Susie glanced across at them and Shadow saw the panic and fear in her eyes.

"Cut the engine. We're going to capsize her," he shouted.

Jimmy, not being used to boats, tried to break the connection, but instead revved the engine and sent them veering closer to the rowing boat. All of a sudden it tipped over. There was a scream as Susie was thrown into the river. Shadow grabbed the life belt and threw it towards her, but she pushed it aside and instead began to swim away.

"Don't be a fool! The current's too strong!" Shadow yelled.

Jimmy immediately pulled off his jacket and shoes and jumped in after her. To Shadow's surprise, his sergeant was a strong swimmer. He had almost caught up with her, when Susie turned around and slashed at him with the pruning shears that were still dangling from her wrist. Shadow heard Jimmy yelp in pain, then there were two loud splashes from the riverbank. Missy, then Jake had launched themselves into the river and were now swimming towards Susie.

She continued thrashing around wildly at Jimmy, and then Jake, as he got closer. Both men tried to grab her without getting cut. Suddenly, Susie shrieked out in pain, as Shadow saw Missy sink her teeth into Susie's right arm. She let go of the pruning shears and Jimmy quickly grabbed her arm. Together with Jake, he managed to get her to the riverbank, where uniformed officers and paramedics were waiting. They hauled her out. Coughing and spluttering she was taken over to the waiting ambulance.

Shadow managed to manoeuvre the little motorboat to the riverbank and awkwardly clambered out. A dripping wet Jimmy and Jake were each huddled, shivering under blankets, as an excited Missy bounced around shaking herself dry over everyone. Shadow turned towards the stretcher where Susie lay exhausted and bleeding, but before he could reach her, he was pushed roughly out of the way by Luke. His face was pale and expressionless as he looked down at the woman he had shared his life with for over thirty years.

"How could you do it?" he asked, his voice barely more than a whisper. "She was the love of my life. How could you take her from me?"

"I just wanted us to be together. I knew I could make you happy," Susie pleaded trying to raise herself up and pushing away the paramedic, who was dressing her wounded leg. "You just needed a chance to see it."

Luke shook his head slowly, his eyes blank, as if he couldn't even see her anymore.

"She was the love of my life," he repeated and then slowly he walked away without a second glance.

"Luke!" screamed Susie, her usually pretty features, contorted and ugly. As he disappeared into the distance, her wails of horror grew louder than the sirens.

SHADOW RESTED HIS head against the cool hospital wall. He wasn't sure if it was the smell of the place or his still-throbbing bruise that was making him feel sick. The plastic chair was hard and uncomfortable. He wanted nothing more than to go back to *Florence* and lie in his bed, but he and Jimmy had to wait until Susie was declared fit to be questioned. He thought of the last words he'd heard Ruth speak. Summer's lease had been too short for both Fay and Emma, and now time had finally run out for Susie.

The squelch from his sergeant's still-wet trainers echoed down the corridor as he returned from his trip to the coffee machine. Jake had refused to be parted from Missy by coming to the hospital to be checked over, so Shadow had arranged for the two of them to be taken to the station where they could get dry and be given something warm to eat. Jimmy handed Shadow a plastic cup and sank down into the chair next to him. They both took a sip and grimaced, Jimmy from the taste and Shadow from the temperature.

"So, how long have you been tracking my mobile?" asked Shadow.

"About two days after I started working for you. When I realised you had no intention of ever letting me know where you were going or answering any of my calls."

Shadow thought back to the night when they had shared a drink with Sophie in The Duke of York.

"Did Sophie know?" he asked.

Jimmy nodded. "Yes, she said I shouldn't take it personally and that you used to completely ignore Barnfather too before he emigrated."

"I see," sighed Shadow. "Well, perhaps I should keep my phone turned on a bit more."

"That would be good." Jimmy smiled. "Maybe even answer it once in a while."

"Don't push it!" Shadow grinned.

Both men sipped their coffee in silence for a few moments. Two nurses wheeled an empty trolley past.

"When did you first suspect Susie, sir?"

Shadow sighed and shook his head. "I don't think you could say I suspected her exactly, but from our first meeting I realised she wasn't quite what she seemed. Maybe I was a little starstruck and the problem was she was so charming, compared to all the other suspects. She fooled me." He paused, still angry with himself, but realised his sergeant was waiting for him to continue with his explanation.

"There were a few things that didn't quite ring true. She told us Fay was almost like family, but she was prepared to let a young, vulnerable girl sleep on the streets. Now of course, I realise she probably didn't turn Fay away completely. I think she told Fay exactly the spot she should go to, telling her she'd be along later with the vodka and more blankets. Maybe even suggesting Fay could come and stay at Granary Court, when Luke was asleep.

"Then there was the whole vegan thing. The fact she still kept chickens and bought the Holy Cow vodka. It was because she didn't really believe it. She was merely pretending, to keep Luke happy.

"It first occurred to me that she might have been involved in Emma's death because of something Oliver said.

When he pulled Susie out of the river, he said she was holding on to a wooden oar. Why would she pick up an oar before jumping in? Was it to keep her afloat or to hold out to her friend? Or, was it because she wanted to wash off the blood?"

Recognition dawned on Jimmy's face. "Emma was hit twice, with something large and flat and something smaller and round. The oar paddle and handle." Shadow nodded, but Jimmy looked confused again. "So when she told everyone she had heard Emma fall in the river, really she had killed her and dragged her body into the tunnel. That was a hell of a risk to take, sir."

"I would put it down to the arrogance of youth. Susie, Emma and Luke were all high achievers, who were used to things going their way. Why wouldn't everyone believe a distraught Susie when she told them her best friend had fallen in the river? Don't forget, if things went wrong, Susie also knew there were others in the area, suspicion might fall on: Oliver, Ruth and Stather."

"I still don't know why she killed Emma. Like you said, they were meant to be best friends."

"That's simple. Susie was jealous of her and particularly her relationship with Luke, who she was almost obsessively in love with herself. For a girl like Susie, who so desperately wanted to be a star, to be constantly outshone must have been torture. She thought with Emma out of the way, she could take her place as the most talented girl in the college and most importantly with Luke. It worked too. She achieved success and fame and in her eyes the most coveted prize of all, being Luke's girlfriend. Like she said to me, he always comes round in the end.

"After that almost everything she did was to keep him happy, from not touring America to turning vegan. She had everything she wanted, then without warning Ruth reappeared and she couldn't risk her saying something to spoil it all. I think Mandy's petition against the soup kitchen gave her the idea to make it look like someone was targeting the homeless. Maybe Jess mentioned that the Holy Cow vodka was at Ted's Bar to her, so she decided to use that to hide the poison. Then it was simply a case of waiting for the right time."

"Like a night when Fay couldn't stay at The Haven and then right after everyone had heard Eric and Mandy complaining loudly about the homeless at the soup kitchen?"

"Precisely. She decided then that was the time to target Ruth and Norman. She even had the rubber gloves on that would later protect her hands and make sure there were no prints. All she had to do was collect the poisoned bottles she'd prepared from her apartment."

"So Ruth knew Susie killed Emma?"

"Not exactly. You see Ruth was standing on the balcony, supposedly acting as a lookout for Stather, but she would have been able to see the river. She would have known Emma didn't fall in but instead returned to the boathouse with Susie. She didn't know what to do. If she said she'd lied in her statement she would get into trouble. If she mentioned the tunnel Stather would lose his job and Susie was very convincing. Killing Fay, Norman and Ruth, it was all to cover up the fact she had killed Emma. New sins to hide an old one. The fact that so many thought she was a good person made it easy for her. Norman even called her an angel, straight after she had made sure she knew where he would be sleeping that night, just as she did with Fay.

"When later she turned up with a bottle of vodka for them, they must have thought it was an act of kindness. Ruth was one of the few who didn't trust her, so Susie had to force the poor woman to drink it."

"And what about the anonymous note you received?"

"Susie sent it. I think she wanted to try and frame Oliver, by making it look like he sent the note suggesting Luke was the murder. She must have realised we would link Ruth and Emma's deaths and we needed to arrest somebody. That's why she made a point of telling me Oliver was jealous of his sister. I think when Luke cut his wrist in Oliver's office, she took the opportunity to take the magazines and paper marked with Luke's blood while Oliver was busy attending to his friend. We should have listened to your sister Angela when she said it was weird Susie was the last person to see Fay and Emma alive. She was right."

Jimmy looked horrified. "Oh God, you won't tell her that will you, sir? She'll be unbearable."

Shadow laughed. "Not if you don't want me to, Sergeant."

They both took a sip of the terrible coffee.

"Actually, it's quite ironic if you think about it, sir. Jake, who saw straight through Susie as well, saved her from drowning, which is what she tried to convince everyone had happened to Emma."

"Almost as ironic as me being the officer to investigate the case."

"How do you mean, sir?"

"Have you never heard the expression, old sins cast a long shadow, Sergeant?"

THE END

If you enjoyed *A Long Shadow*, please support the author and leave a review!

Join Tule Publishing's newsletter for more great reads and weekly deals!

If you enjoyed *A Long Shadow,*
you'll love the next book in….

THE CHIEF INSPECTOR SHADOW SERIES

Book 1: *A Long Shadow*

Book 2: *A Viking's Shadow*
Coming August 2021!

Available now at your favorite online retailer!

ABOUT THE AUTHOR

H L Marsay always loved detective stories and promised herself that one day, she would write one too. She is lucky enough to live in York, a city full of history and mystery. When not writing, the five men in her life keep her busy – two sons, two dogs and one husband.

REFERENCES

The two lines of poetry quoted by Ruth Brooke
are from "Solitude" by Ella Wheeler Wilcox
and "Sonnet 18" by William Shakespeare.

A Long Shadow Crossword

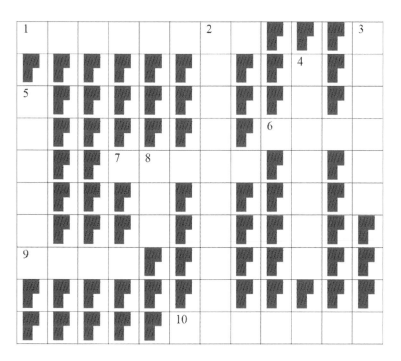

Across

1. Wishing they had Sarah's luck, initially makes Jane, Emily and Anne feel lousy (8 letters)

6. This gateau is better if Luca keeps it (4 letters)

7. Vote often despite Kremlin's authority—that's the spirit! (5 letters)

9. Amore—that romance isn't in English (4 letters)

10. Getting the wrong idea in NYC can be deadly (7 letters)

Down

2. By going through the narrow passage, the lackey wins his prize (10 letters)

3. Partly redefining a close ally (6 letters)

4. By making a blackboard he relates better to pupils (6 letters)

5. Let the nun go underground (6 letters)

8. Rowing at home makes almost half board a better idea (3 letters)

A LONG SHADOW CROSSWORD – SOLUTION

1 J	E	A	L	O	U	2 S	Y	■	■	3 F
■	■	■	■	■	N	■	■	4 S	■	R
5 T	■	■	■	■	I	■	■	L	■	I
U	■	■	■	■	C	■	6 C	A	K	E
N	■	7 V	8 O	D	K	A	■	T	■	N
N	■	■	A	■	E	■	■	E	■	D
E	■	■	R	■	L	■	■	R	■	■
9 L	O	V	E	■	W	■	■	■	■	■
■	■	■	■	■	A	■	■	■	■	■
■	■	■	■	10 C	Y	A	N	I	D	E

Thank you for reading

A LONG SHADOW

If you enjoyed this book, you can find more from all our great authors at TulePublishing.com, or from your favorite online retailer.

TULE
PUBLISHING

Printed in Great Britain
by Amazon